I0582721

# Conversational THERAPY

## STORIES AND PLAYS

# NICK VORO

I dedicate this book to my loving parents (Elena & Yuriy), who have always kept my dreams alive. The first people to refer to me as a "writer." The same kind-hearted mother and father who bought me my first writing desk, a new computer, and creative writing guidebooks to start me on my journey. A big thank you from the bottom of my heart.

A special thank you also to my grandfather Alexander and grandmother Viktoria for always being there for me. I am forever grateful for their love and care, unforgettable summers at the dacha and our memorable trip to Egypt.

It would be very remiss of me to forget my gorgeous wife Sue and to not thank her for thinking all art is pretentious (with some luck this book will turn you into an art aficionado), and I would be equally remiss to not thank my cherub-faced daughter Juliet and her vehement disregard for bedtime—your nocturnal fighting spirit added to the long gestation period of this book but it also made it so much better.

And in loving memory of my grandmother Natalia (a skilled chef, an amazing baker, and the woman who tirelessly spent hours reading books to me over the phone) and my uncle Dmitriy (forever my friend, a knowledgeable historian, my tour guide of

Ukraine and the first person to introduce me to a computer) and my grandfather Alexander (an expert fisherman who taught me how to hold a fishing rod sturdy, an early riser and the first person to greet me in the mornings). My love for all of you did not just suddenly vanish just because you are not here. In fact, it is even stronger. My love for both of you did not just suddenly vanish just because you are not here. In fact, it is even stronger.

*Nick, July 3, 2022*

# TABLE OF CONTENTS

NICK VORO DOES NOT EXIST. Now yes, I know, that's an odd thing to write, seeing that this is the Introduction to *Conservational Therapist*, a fabulous 'first-timer' (wink) collection of short fiction and plays. If *he* doesn't exist, you exclaim, how does this *book* exist? So you reread the author bio, you fervidly flip ahead to the grateful note of thanks this "Nick" has written to his loved ones, veritable Vespers of veneration, and ask, Isn't that proof enough?

You, I believe, like many others, have been duped. Now I don't want to be Harsch, or make this too much about myself, but I believe it's *important* to not be duped. Dupes do not make it far in the world. Dupes often end up on the street, shattered and disillusioned. Beggars to society.

So let's not be duped, alright?

I was introduced to "Nick Voro" on the social media platform known as Goodreads, where not all the reads are good, where "he" was posing as an admirer of the *very much real* and revered author Joseph McElroy. The context around that interaction eludes me, but eventually this Voro fessed up to being a writer of some talent and, being an editor, which I do not claim to be, but am, I suggested taking a look at a few odds and ends of his efforts.

Yes, I was trolling, or trawling, for clients. To this point I had snatched up Goodreads plebes from

A-U, preferring to do things alphabetically due to my lifelong ABCOCD. Thus, I needed a V. The Author Claiming to be Nick, whom I now believe had 'nicked' this name, offered to send the varied and inchoate stories that would make up this aforementioned first book, *Conversing Theremin*.

Upon reading these fictions, I was struck, right in the gut, where all my flabber is ghasted. I was struck by the boldness of vision, sure, and the concatenation of themes and characters, yet there was something distinctly *chimerical* about this wordy beast. Some stories were raw, others polished. Some stories were comical, others dark with nary a laugh to be disinterred. A story felt European, another American, or syrupy *Canadian*.

I, who read millions of words each year, felt a pricking of my neck hairs. This didn't add up. My 'dupe' alert rang red.

After much thought, and a few logical equations, I hereby propose that Nick Voro is comprised of three writers, whom I will call Albert, Barry, and Charlie.

Albert masters the noir. We sit in the dingy dark with Albert during "The Trolley Car Ride", "Murder on the Christmas Express," and "The Lonely Motel."

Barry weeps words of the sentimental. Our hearts wilt whilst reading "A Keepsake Melody",

"The Last Laugher", and the short theatre piece, "Crass Distinction."

Charlie, well he's demilord of the metafictional! Charlie worms through every passage in the creative fabric, like the hole in the motel wall, linking each story and play to the numinous.

Oh, they try to match each other's form here and there, willy and nilly, try to throw you off the trail, but it was not fooling this reader. Why then, you wonder, did they seek an editor? Soft hearted, you may think that they, as 'Nick', needed an extra set of eyes, someone to stich this literary ragdoll together. That's sweet. Or perhaps, even better, they placed bets? Will we be found out? Albert, he gambled everything.

Poor Albert.

Voro, from the Latin *Devore*—to swallow, devour.

Hook, line and no-thinker.

Are you not convinced? No? If it's still 2022, head to that pictorial playground, Instagram. Nick Voro, you'll see, or won't see, is merely a fine suit and some handsome shoes. This man posing as Nick is a hand-model! (Wonderful hands, I must say.) Try Facebook? Nothing. Meta-farce! That face-feast YouTube brings up a distorted image, *c'est tout, mes amis*, and when discussing a three-way Zoomalong launch—a frickin' launch, pals—of our coronal samidzats—"Nick," Bursey and me—guess who demurred?

Cough cough, can't make it. Too shy. Must manicure. *Usw.*

But does any of this matter? *Doesn't the work* —no, shut up! Of course it does! The world is full of dupes; everywhere I turn, here a dupe there a dupe. Still, I suppose I should flip this on its side, give it a spin, make it dizzy, provide something quotable beyond 'miraculous editing in this Cerberus-scribed invention!" I do, after all, prefer to retain my clients.

So here:

This collection, *Consternated Threnody* by Nick Voro, is a worthy addition to any Library for Dupes, a deceitful book that shall sit alongside that esteemed shelf in every discerning reader's bibliothèque, that dusty recessoir for those most mysterious and untraceable of authors, the vanished, the mythical, the Elena Ferrentes, the W.D. Clarkes, the Pynchons, Travens, and Daras... and now—*note the plural* —the Nick Voros.

Albert, Barry, and Charlie.
Enjoy!

Lee D. Thompson
Editor, author, not-a-dupe

# ALLIGATOR RESORT

I AM A SARCASTIC ASSHOLE with a mocking sense of humor. I am also a user of people. Usually those closest to me. I collect their personal information. I drain them. Among all the well-known things a friend or a lover does, I go a step further, and do what one should never do— take what I am told in utter confidence and use it against the very people who have told it to me.

Yes, I am perfectly sane, fully aware of my

actions. Nothing is ever done in a moment of estrangement from self, or capricious lapsing into passion. I know what I am doing and why I am doing it, I understand the consequences, and yet I carry on.

This is real life after all, and there will always be casualties. So whether strangers, vaguely familiar acquaintances I met at some cocktail party, childhood friends with whom I played croquet on their father's newly-acquired estate's lawn, or spent semesters roomed up with in the same Harvard dorm, all that ceases to matter as they become my informants (non-consensual and without a formal agreement, of course), adding that touch of authenticity to my grandiose projects.

The realization of treachery and betrayal only sinks in after they read my latest bestseller (name change being only a preventative measure until they inevitably catch on) and see their private lives publicly broadcast, accessible to anyone willing to spend a few bucks to fulfill a voyeuristic characteristic everyone has (no matter how seemingly different we are from one another). I copyright their lives as a figment of my boundless artistic imagination, which I use—albeit at a very leisurely pace—to produce original albeit slightly fabricated imitations of life.

If my publishers only knew... Well, even then I doubt they would care, as long as this information didn't leak to the press (I seal my lips). Because if it did, that is a stock-market-crash slide in sales and a bunch of lawsuits I hardly want to deal with. I am imagining they probably do not either. My lawyer fees alone would be an extravagant figure with plenty of zeros, conceivably the sum total of my last three publishing-house paychecks. I might be rich, but no one is rich enough for a lawyer's blood.

So, I finish this confession to my psychiatrist (talking to clinicians in confined spaces solves a good deal of what is left unsaid in the wide-open spaces of real life... usually), stating that the dust jackets of my novels denounce any real-life connections. And you know what he says? Nothing.

Absolutely nothing. Yellow pad in hand, he simply continues to scribble a Picasso-worthy sketch with a watercolor pencil.

I am neither a fortune-teller nor am I as intuitive as a woman, but looking at the latest vessel spread in the *Yachting Magazine* lying open on his mahogany desk, I can only assume it's a sketch of his next boat. Or the one he already owns, and now he is compulsively comparing, sketch-filling in its shortcomings, which he has realized while window shopping other lusciously illustrated yachts just slightly out of his price range.

He has no answers for me. No solutions for any of my problems. On a good note, he has a suggestion. He recommends heartily that I take a vacation, which he himself is going to do soon— probably sail around the world on his yacht.

But who am I to judge; I should be frank and say these mind-stabilizing sessions are paid for by my parents. They sponsor most of my lifestyle, including paying for my aristocratic downtown loft, thinking my job to be more of a hobby than someone's actual life's work. My personal cash-caretakers with hearts of financial gold. Their digit, no-strings-attached love knows few boundaries and their monthly allowances keep me afloat even though I can keep myself afloat. The best part: my amassed literary fortune keeps growing, bypassing the usual lifestyle reductions thanks to the willing nature of these parental units. A win-win for everyone.

I take a minute to ponder this near-mute medical practitioner's getaway suggestion and come up with the perfect spot—the family cottages. As they say, "If you can't face your problems, run away."

A few days later, I am in the back seat of my parents' first bought car, before their ascent to status—a Volkswagen Beetle—a crammed criminally compact car created at the behest of the German Führer (with his expansion and enslavement plans for much of Europe, I am baffled he did not design a roomier auto). So much for running…

Most would attribute my father's choice to hold on to the mint 1970s vehicle as a sign of nostalgia, a humbling reminder of one's roots no matter how high you climb. The reality is much simpler. My father has never thrown out a single thing in his life, living his all-American hoarding dream. And so we were off in the hoarder's vehicle of choice toward a perfectly idyllic location for some well-deserved recreational rest.

I know it sounds rather ridiculous, but I am not even dressed properly—Armani sports jacket and Gucci loafers. What a nightmare. My multi-millionaire banker father gripping the steering wheel and next to him Mother, who has her own cooking show, with some underhanded feminist views. A plagiaristic Bestselling Author, a Shady Banker, and a Television Personality slash Leading Activist for women's lib—the *Three's Company* gang from cable reruns with one sex reassignment surgery for the analogy to work and minus the edgy late-70s double entendres riding around in the Führer's sardine can of a car.

An indefinite period later (that feels like an eternity), we arrive and blessedly I no longer have to listen to Mother hum Janis Joplin songs and Father make frequent urgent phone calls to his business partner (who is probably his mistress).

As I step out of the car, fresh air rushes upward my nose. Air virginal and undefiled by large fossil fuel companies and their steady climate-changing contributions. This freshness is new to me. I am a city dweller after all, used to ensconcing in darkness, breathing pollutants and ingesting Schedule II drugs.

My most reoccurring imagery is of neon-lit warehouses where the next your-presence-is-required party is happening. Where glow sticks make up for a vital assembly-stic part of some probably underage girl's latest Nicole Miller two-piece.

I feel claustrophobic among the ancient giants, the natural force of Mother Nature overwhelming me, agitating the remnants of illegally obtained substances still coursing through my bloodstream. I feel a gravitational pull. Invisible forces seize hold of my soul and tear it from my body, leaving behind just the shell, cadaverous and incomplete.

No matter where I have gone my whole life, I have always felt a violent pressure to fit in, projecting something I am not through a made-up personality. Here I am compelled to confront a part of me I left behind—my innocent adolescence.

What strange revelations fresh air can have on a person. Here in the heartland of America, in its woods, I suddenly feel nostalgia for my childhood. Surely there is a secret foundry, hidden deep in the forest, releasing scents of sentimentality, evoking the alluring recollection of some Camp Scout's burnt marshmallows...

The following afternoon I awake in my old room, confronted by dusty bookshelves and monstrous stuffed animals. I lie in bed recollecting the past evening with my father, his prolonged attempt to ignite a campfire. Okay, so he did not strike two rocks belonging to the flint family—Aristocrats and Neanderthals are vastly different groups after all, belonging to different social classes. He still did better than I ever thought possible, and I applauded his efforts all the same for even mustering enough interest to attempt this. I shift my thoughts back to myself (how typical). My body aches from a contorted sleeping position, my vision is blurry and my fingers are cramping with what must be early signs of arthritis. On top of this laundry list of complaints, I have a full bladder from all the imported beer last night. Not a good start to the day.

So while in the bathroom taking care of that unsavory business a man of letters should never be overly explicit about in his writing unless toilet humor makes a grand comeback, I happen to look out the window to witness a congregation—don't ask me for quantitative data, I didn't count them—of alligators slithering on the meticulously manicured lawn below and dirtying the adjacent ultramarine lake (and its esteemed crystal-clear clarity) with their predominating greenery, causing me to stare in sheer disbelief from this modernistic chic cabin erected by a renowned architect who had a penchant for taking your ideas, completely disregarding them and delivering a building tailored to his own vision—a building that is aesthetically pleasing but completely useless as a stronghold.

I steadily back away from the window, back to the present moment, utterly horrified by my current predicament.

The corner of my right eye catches sight of the living room's doorframe, the safety of another room making me relax prematurely. Then the same eye catches another sight, the sight of a Cloaked Figure lurking down the hallway.

If anyone ever wanted an accurate depiction of the Grim Reaper, this guy was the personification of Death. Bloodshot bulging eyes, jet black hair matted with sweat, and body draped in black with extremely pale hands and grossly protruding veins.

Around his waist is a leather belt with a

holster housing a positively menacing handgun, possibly a Beretta, known for its deadly accuracy and relentless reliability (but this is just a guess from a non-gun enthusiast and First Amendment gospeler).

I want to call him fraudulent, a product of a make-believe world, an embodiment of my worst fears, but his presence quickly cripples me with an overspreading sensation of dread.

My head begins to throb, the once-safe living room becomes noticeably hotter, even scorching, and I feel a blinding notion enter my mind: purification from sin is through punishment, and he is here to punish me (and therefore save me).

Eventually, I reject the momentary proselytism spurred by this escapee from the nether regions, come to and sprint for the bathroom, bolting the door, entrusting my life to a flimsy lock (avant-garde architects never do seem to care for security).

Outstanding; simply outstanding! Singled out and confined to my bathroom, incredulous as I overlook a gator wasteland, a reptile-strewn lawn leading to a single road that is the only direct passageway to my parents' cabin, unless of course I feel a surge of heroism and act on my parallel alternative of making it safely across the lake by canoe (my parents sojourn at a much swankier cabin across the lake, one designed by a much superior architect I might add)... but surely once I get a paddle in the water, they will grab me and haul my body with their powerfully sharp jaws into the murky depths of the lake, suffocation by immersion, expelling what remaining oxygen I have and submerging, submerging....

A knock interrupts my fleeting sinking feeling and horrible visions of frantic paddling, alligators ramming, a capsized canoe and gut-wrenching human screams for help in gator-infested waters. My passing thought: at least he has enough manners to knock. And since I fail to ask him in, as should come as no great surprise, the pounding only intensifies, with his fist now connecting with the door. He never even bothers with the handle.

Either he knows better, or... he knows me. In the grand scheme of things, believability already stretching to the snapping point, could he not be one of those I depleted, stole from, drained? One of those I have used and flung away? Someone whose trust I betrayed, breaking the inviolable rule of every strong and true friendship? And has this violation, betrayal, alienation, perhaps induced such profound hurt to cause the donning of a *cloche*? Have I pushed a man to conceive a devious plan with devilish determination to end the orderly life of a best-selling life-plagiarizing novelist? The door shudders, its laborious life of constantly opening and closing coming to an end. I brace myself. Any moment now it will concede defeat to this bestial besieging. His foot is obviously at work here. Delivering impassioned declarative kicks. The door moves inward, putting pressure on the hinges. Yes, yes, any moment now. My beacon of hope will plunge into darkness. I need divine inspiration. I need something... soon... instantaneously. I am inexperienced with the whole survival-tactic routine, cognizant that this makes me the wrong candidate for the job. But this hindrance greatly affects my inheritance. And I must, at all costs, prolong my existence long enough to cash my parents' life insurance policy. I will not allow disinheritance through premature death.

With the policy as a motivational driver, I step to the window casement. I place one foot firmly on the bathtub, boost myself up and sit down on the ledge of the window. The bathroom door keeps shuddering, about to disintegrate, taking numerous kicks from the Cloaked Figure, who apparently has the legs of a bodybuilder and the feet of a football hooligan.

I open the window and swing my feet over.

The ground below overflows with alligators. Now I am not an expert, but these alligators seem larger than your typical swamp dweller and their hostility spurred on by something other than biology, and if I take a real wild guess, I will say it is achieved by a chemical reaction from some good ole human tampering with Mother Nature.

I start edging along the slopped shingled roof of the third story toward the downspout to the right, remaining aware that if I slip, they will devour me. These loathsome reptilians. They seem to sense me and move about anxiously, replicating my movements perfectly. True to their predatory nature, their movements are almost noiseless, making you momentarily forget they are there until you look down and confirm the nightmare is real.

In the distance, I spot my canoe, a swaying siren, tempting me aboard. But it might as well be a mirage. I shake my head. I have no illusions about using it. They can keep up just fine, before ramming and overtaking. I double down on my efforts, believing in no other alternative path.

Our repetition of movement evolves into a rhythm of sorts—I crawl, they mimic; I speed up; they adjust their pace accordingly, my circling copies, tailing me in a never-ending cycle until I have this thought, lose concentration, mentally slip, lose footing, and physically slide, emitting a vigorous cry for help that creeps upwards from the pit of my stomach and through my windpipe, a musical composition to accompany my descent while the whole time clawing at the shingles until I catch hold of the gutter at the last possible minute, scrape one hand in the process and helplessly hang there holding on for dear dear life with the other, increasingly trembling and rapidly perspiring.

I feel blood oozing from the cuts on my free-floating hand, dribbling down and exciting the horde below. My other hand is slipping, my arm muscles tightening up. I cannot hold my weight much longer considering my current physical condition, not to mention years of lackluster parenting lacking any actual parental advice, formative years without direction, without those early nuggets of wisdom regarding my future life-sustaining-needs in case of possible survival situations, all leaving me completely unprepared to deal with situations like my present predicament where I am called upon to perform one-arm gutter gymnastics and easily swing my way across to safety.

A sharp *bang* explodes behind me, but before I can react, something pierces my shoulder as it travels past my left ear. Upon closer examination, I pronounce it to be a bullet, surpassing the speed of sound and passing through the shooting gallery placard, a.k.a. my shoulder, before embedding itself in the framework of the house. A bullet meaning to take my life. Oh, great! Now he is shooting at me.

For some reason I expected him to follow me through the bathroom window, but he has to be on the ground below, shooting up while I swing around perfectly posed in his crosshairs, readying for my headshot feature on the cover of *Shingle Shenanigans*.

*Click*. He does not wait long before he fires the weapon again. The next bullet pierces the previously grazed shoulder and causes me to swing forward from the sheer impact of the projectile.

Third time being the charm, and considering

it is a lonely place at the top, I swing forward with what little remains of my strength, plunge forth like a trapeze artist with hope for the best, and land ungracefully on the deck of the second floor, smacking my head.

My thunderous fall initiates an advancing footrace below—what beasts were still in the nearby water now all touch ground, and those already on land rapidly round the corner of the cottage toward the stairs, toward me. A race for the gnawing of the human meat (that's me). I quickly get to my feet; in my head a nightingale is singing its morbid song, announcing my inevitable death. The weapon discharges again. Time is clearly not on my side. I start to run, sprint forward with a marathon runner's finish-line determination, beat the beasts to the side stairs and only come to a full stop once the ancient forest giants with their crowns of green hide me from projectiles and snapping jaws.

The pain I feel is excruciating, spoiling clear-headed thinking, distorting, jumbling all the thoughts inside my head. All I know is I must keep moving. Stopping is not on the itinerary. I must remain in constant motion. It is integral to my survival.

I am also leaving behind a trail the Cloaked Figure will find easy enough to track. I dismiss praying. A silent and unseen god will not answer my payers. He will not pardon me the grim reality of wandering through these labyrinthine trails waiting for the Cloaked Figure or his hell spawn to materialize.

Blindly walking forward, focusing on some imaginary point—when it is all just trees and more trees—I miss the ones that matter: the trees painted to mark a muddy area ahead. And one lame step later, all that it takes before the ground turns to soft wet earth and my legs start to descend into this suffocating sludge.

I have the sinking vision of my sunken body decomposing in the mud, preserved for eternity down to the finest details, such as my grimace of horrid fright. Until, one day, a forester stumbles across my perfectly preserved body, a rare find, a grotesque curiosity destined for a display case at a national museum.

The noise of approaching footsteps, human and alligatorian, breaks my useful reverie. The abundance of trees nearby is my only hope. As I unbuckle my belt, further visions invade my mind, a cluster of invasive, agonizing thoughts. Some involve dismemberment while other frightening flash-forward scenarios focus on evisceration. With terror in my eyes, and a terrible tremor in my hands, and with my personal best rendition of the cool technique of the Marlboro Man, I aim the lasso—my belt, extending into the buckle—as accurately as possible toward a vertical crack in the nearest tree.

I cannot hold back my surprise when it actually works. The buckle, a metallic clasp custom-fitted for the crevice! I give it a firm tug, securing it in place. Then I yank with my good hand, dragging myself out, decreasing the distance to refuge literally one handful at a time.

Once out, I take painstakingly slow steps down a concealed path, encountering my first bit of good luck by coming across an old barn with loosely-hung wide-open doors revealing a Chevrolet pickup rust-box inside. The only research I have ever done for any of my novels (outside of pumping my friends for personal bits of information) was for a pulp novel where the lead character had to hot-wire a car. I put that knowledge to good use. It takes a bit, the starter turns, smoke spews out the exhaust, but eventually a thunderously rattling noise sounds as the engine reanimates (similar to the spark that gave life to Victor Frankenstein's misunderstood monstrous creation). I have no idea why it is there, but I am thankful it is.

I cling to the steering wheel with my trembling hands and back out, turn and head down an L-shaped road. As I round the corner, I experience a sudden bout of paralysis. Ahead, bent at one knee, is the Cloaked Figure, his arms now gripping a state-of-the-art rifle, which he points at my windshield.

I shift to a lower gear and floor it. The Chevrolet races forward as the windshield begins taking direct, silent hits, fracturing as I impassively pierce through his body, all the while sonically imagining the sickening crunch of his bones breaking as he slides below. The truck momentarily lifts, rocking all over the place, passing over the human roadside bump. I fix my eyes on the vastness ahead, never bothering to look back.

With the sun setting, I turn on the headlights. My parents' cabin is not much farther. I can feel the closeness of my destination when, without warning, a jolt forces the old Chevrolet from the forest road. I try my best to compensate for the sudden directional change, but my reflexive steering still results in a head-on collision with a tree.

This development is not in my favor! In fact, the situation is a touch demoralizing. The driver's-side door, taking the full force of a massive alligator's armor-plated tail (as I have now registered), will not budge.

I find myself imprisoned inside a rusting

coffin with commotion all around, courtesy of the swiftly approaching, ravenous, blood-lusting and continuously charging bastard offspring (now that their father, the perpetrator of all this madness, is dead).

A second hit, this time from a different alligator's tail, crushes the passenger door inward. The window dissolves into shards, imploding, puncturing my skin and creating a passageway for a large grotesque head with a salivating mouth. I am covered in blood, choking on it, wanting to give up. But now is not the time to play the role of a sniveling victim airing out all his complaints.

I leap, land on the backseat, rotate my body and start frantically kicking at the rear window until I feel it give. With vigor for survival, I thrust my body through the broken opening, tumble out of the truck's bed and, alligators at my heels, run until I reach my parents' cabin.

The air inside is otherworldly, as if it carries particles responsible for overstimulating these deranged peninsula inhabitants on this fine summer day.

My search of the cottage yields no one. I look out the window expecting the cabin to be surrounded, but there are no gators anywhere. I am alone guarding the fortress, waiting for the Tartars to show up. I open a few windows, allowing fresh air to circulate. Then I sit down, feeling the full force of my exhaustion and my injuries. The adrenaline is wearing off, pain returning. Is it so preposterous to imagine that the mysterious and sinister mastermind, the Cloaked Figure, would abduct my parents and deliver an army of supercharged alligators to my cottage for the sole purpose of testing an immature, egotistical coward? Or am I over-complicating the matter and he simply did not care, fully expecting me not to have made it out alive from the cottage's bathroom?

Trapped again. I need someone... anyone... to come to rescue me (after my futile attempt at rescuing others). I need someone to answer the unexplainable.

Just then, the phone rings.

It is the mismatched married couple from my

favorite sitcom: My Life. And while, my alive-and-well parents talk about everything they bought while shopping in town, never bothering to ask why exactly I am at their cottage, my thoughts are on their life insurance policy, the structural damage to my cabin and the cloak coming away from the maniac's face the moment I hit him with the junker truck; regrettably never fully exposing his face, but more of that matted jet black hair initially revealed during the bathroom ambush. At one point, it even parted, further revealing scalp scarring.

I know that pitch-black hair with the striking scar underneath... And that is not the only thing I know.

I also know he is here. In the room with me. I sense him standing to the side of me, covered in his own blood. I slowly turn to face him, instantaneously proving myself right, a victor and loser at the same moment.

My eyes wander over to his holster. It is empty. His gun seems to be missing. This somewhat reduces the threat.

Along with his missing gun, his cloak is torn to shreds. Is it from the truck swipe or his children turning on their maker, sensing a shift in power? Spotting weakness in an impenetrable tyrannical ruler?

He allows me to continue my restless roaming across his body while he just stands there, in one spot, a motionless monolith, a dark brooding figure, as blood drips down on to the floor, a soothing sort of dripping, leaving stains which will endure at least a couple of cleanings.

Slowly, and with trembling hands, I decide to remove his cloak. I do just that. The purpose behind my actions unknown even to me. Perhaps it is the glimpse of my killer's face, a confirmation of his identity before he slaughters me without a second thought.

The cloak falls behind his head, drapes his shoulders.

Underneath, a yacht is visibly bracing against high winds and stormy sea. It looks abandoned. Unmanned. It is struggling to stay afloat. A tragic sight. One I cannot look away from. I stand and stare as darkness steadily eclipses everything until nothing remains. Not him nor I.

# A KEEPSAKE MEMORY

I HAVE TO HAND IT TO THEM—they were efficient. In spite of my pleadings, I not only dressed but packed my suitcase and somehow quieted down long enough to follow their diplomatic order of things.

They were professional, government-sanctioned agents (or so their inner pocketed badges pronounced them to be), and I was just a civilian without their security clearance or level of expertise.

They sandwiched me once we merged with the foot traffic in the corridor outside of my hospital room, one on either side applying just enough bodily pressure for me not to forget they were there.

Not a soul gave us a passing look. That is how superbly they conducted themselves, how perfectly they blended in with their immediate environment. And honestly, I could not knock their treatment of me—just a pair of friendly chaperones transporting a teenage girl through the hospital.

This was not meant to last. Outside, in the parking lot, as we approached an unmarked white van, they tased me with devilish synchronicity. Electricity shot through me. I was weightless, seemingly suspended in midair before they put me down on the armored-plated vehicle's floor.

They instructed me to take a seat on the metal bench molded into the framework of the van and secured my left wrist to a mounted bar running the length of the van. The bracelet pinched and made a very annoying clanging noise. Doors slammed shut and someone outside tapped twice to initiate this unauthorized transfer of human cargo.

The van jolted forward; I slipped off the bench and pain swiftly soared up my imprisoned arm. When I looked down, I noticed specks of blood beginning to appear underneath the shiny metal, which must have been wiped to gleaming perfection with some skin irritating, corrosive substance. It bitterly stung my still-scabbed wrists.

Locked inside this prisoner transport vehicle, I thought about why I was being treated like a war criminal. I probably had my politically correct politician stepfather to thank for that; for teaching a valuable life lesson to his not-yet eighteen and out-of-control teenage daughter, an insignificant little girl standing before a man and a cause (not just a man—a man with a vision; a vision of a Utopia, a New Mesopotamia right on the steps of Capitol Hill).

The unseen driver applied the brake, and the van slowed noticeably. After making one more turn, it came to a halt. The twin-suited brick-armed giants made another appearance, unlocked my fashionable, blood-coated bracelet and brought me out into the light of day.

It took a moment for a city dweller, not to mention an absent-minded one like myself, to acclimatize. A reddish brick structure, a few stories high (unmistakably an abbey), greeted me. It had medieval-looking gates, a giant courtyard, and two tall towers.

The whole thing was misplaced, surrounded by nothing but desert and endless weeds covering the dry, deficient soil. I heard a door slam, the engine start up, and helplessly I watched the van speed away. No one seemed worried about me making a run for it. Why would they worry? Where could I possibly go? With only one option, one path to take, I approached this isolated abomination, made it past the walk-through chain-link fence gate, already unlocked, my arrival plainly anticipated beforehand, and found myself beneath a crimson awning shading the front doors, my hand nervously clutching the handle of the suitcase. I will not deny being awash with dread, terrified to take the first step toward my rehabilitation.

Thankfully, Dr. Brown was there to help me along, a tradesman of commodities, such as favors. You do him one and he does you one back. All he asked of me was to come inside and, in return... well, that I never got to find out. They discovered his partly vermin-mutilated corpse face down in the boiler room three days after I made my miraculous escape and finally got around to phoning in the anonymous tip off.

Once the information was out there, newspapers wasted no time clashing, simultaneously reporting this headliner story:

"Asylum Scandal: One man found dead, presumed to be a doctor, in the boiler room of an abandoned abbey clandestinely converted into an operational medical facility, laying face down with two bullet holes in the back of his head, an execution-style murder according to the detectives assigned to the case. The man's colleague, attired similarly in a white doctor's lab coat, was located upstairs, bloody but alive, crudely tied to a patient's bed and refusing to cooperate with the police, stonewalling the entire active investigation. Foul play is very much suspected. Stay tuned for more information about this broadening scandal."

They handled it very professionally and tastefully I must say, I would have titled it, "Asylum Scandal, or What's a Ph.D. to a Rat," with the first line going something like this, "Boiler room rats have a banquet... dismembering, mutilating and gnawing on a celebrated doctor in the field of..." But this is me acting my own age, showing that bit of immaturity almost expected of me. Newspapers and journalists who write for them are always tactful, even when reporting on grisly murders full of gruesome details. I kept the newspaper around, even as it yellowed and the ink smudged from multiple handling and re-reading. Each time I perused it, I always added my own inventions to the text: "When the police discovered Dr. Brown, they thought he was still alive. Turned out the rodents had gotten underneath him and were rattling his corpse back and forth. According to the lone survivor, a kidnapped underage girl held there against her will, Dr. Brown, had a sway about him when he was still alive."

But I am getting ahead of myself. Let us return to the story at hand:

The room I was staying in did nothing to alter my first impressions of the abbey. A bare-minimum airtight compartment with no proper circulation system installed, smelling disgustingly of hydrogen peroxide.

I also had to face the fact that I did not have storage for all the clothes compressed in my over-brimming suitcase—which was about to detonate, sending cotton, polyester and silk articles in every direction.

What the room did have was a wardrobe, though it lacked a mirror on the inside of the door, whether by the age of the design (it looked antique) or by the fact it failed to meet safety standards and regulations, branded as a weapon that patients could use to harm others or themselves once they have shattered the mirror and extracted their preferred piece from the heap. What a strange sight it must be to see your own face, have it imprinted on your consciousness right before you tatter through some ligaments.

Thankfully, there is always a solution, as long as you stay a few steps ahead of your captors. A window at dusk could alternate as my personal mirror; outside of a slightly askew reflection, it was better than nothing.

Minus the aforementioned bed (or have I not mentioned it? it was a bed; it housed a double mattress with railings on each side), there was also a closet—just don't delude yourself into thinking that it was one of those spacious walk-ins every teenage girl dreams of. It was small. The hangers were plastic (God forbid they would have wire hangers you can untwist and jab into your jugular or wherever else) and suspended from an aluminum crosspiece, which was screwed into the wall.

I guess if you were looking for a place to withdraw in splendorous seclusion, this was it.

Does a premeditated act against yourself make you the victim or the culprit responsible for your own demise?

This great mental debate was going on as a pair of orderlies, only two hours into my stay, forcibly strapped down my still sore wrists. I cannot justify my actions; I had lost control, and instead of sharing remembrances of the damaging episodes that contributed to my present breakdown, I shared the contents of my late breakfast (a glass of orange juice and an English muffin) with Dr. Brown.

So, I could not really blame those orderlies

with their bulging muscles, and their immaculate white uniforms for the carelessness and inhumanity they displayed toward me. This was simply their job.

How else do you deal with regurgitation and hysteria, except with containment and sedation? It was time for the two red pills. I was not too sure what they contained, and I am not too sure now, but I swallowed them under the watchful eye of Dr. Brown.

He stuck around afterward, the last time I would see him. Perhaps I was the last person he saw except, of course, for his killer(s). Lacking clairvoyant abilities, sadly, he simply went about his duties, remaining close, monitoring the effects of the therapeutically-friendly medicine as it calmed what he probably classified in his jotted-down notes as an exhibition of maniacal tendencies.

Every two to four hours, Dr. Brown would good-humoredly signal the second of the two orderlies—after the first one had given me my soon-to-be daily intake of pills and a glass of water to wash them down with—over to my bed-ridden side. The second orderly's finger, encased in a skin-tight latex glove containing baby powder on the inside, would slither bulgingly over my gums, moving down the upper and lower levels of the gumline. He would then ask me to "open wide" in a mechanized voice, one lacking any room for empathy, while shining a thin narrow flashlight down my throat.

When all three parties were satisfied with the digestion of the medication, they left me alone to rest. To them, I may have seemed in stable condition, but in reality I perceived myself as an object, an inanimate object, a hollow revolving cylinder undergoing imminent changes due in-part to rising atmospheric pressure while hopped up on god knows what, fading to coma-like sleep and becoming more and more inaccessible to any further rational thinking.

*

For the rest of that night, and partly the next day, I was heavily sedated. I awoke when the medication finally become more and more ineffectual. I staggered out of bed and tried to focus as I approached the only window in my room, which gave a view of the courtyard.

Staggering to that window felt like the most physically strenuous activity I had done in weeks. Through vertical bars blocking the window, reminding me of my imprisonment, I explored the blurry terrain courtesy of my still adjusting eyes.

The courtyard was empty and unpatrolled but had unmistakably undergone certain changes. Additional "enhancements" were added, retrofitting the empty space with the latest in precautionary measures. The cameras and razor-wire fencing made me think of the time I visited Guantánamo Bay where my stepfather had some shadowy business to conduct involving Pentagon defense contracts (his twisted idea of some sort of father-daughter bonding trip).

A firm knock at the door brought me back, but before I could utter a sound, the stranger barged inside and swept my right hand into his own. After a few brief pumps of a handshake—in the process of which the stranger scrutinized my sutured wrists—he finally introduced himself as Dr. Murray and elaborated on the details of being Dr. Brown's replacement.

He was robust, full of manly vigor. He was someone who took great personal risks in his self-less quest to get to the root of the problem, the nitty-gritty responsible for the distortion of the human psyche. He was not one to just gloss over the problem. No not at all. But the type to make an emotional investment while collaborating with you every step of the way. He absolutely abhorred the much-favored principles and techniques! Instead, he chose diversification and experimentation thus allowing himself to venture into the great depths of the unknown.

Apparently this was how his patients described him, and he decided to quote them. To me, he seemed like a double-faced well-bred hack from an upper-class family, polished to perfection on the outside and perhaps a bit vulgar somewhere deep down. He didn't exactly exude trustworthiness, especially when I had the privilege to sit in the shorter, non-adjustable chair (by comparison to his black leather, pneumatically-operated throne, which was better suited for a corporate executive than someone with a degree in medicine, and which gave him a clear advantage of elevated positioning as his highness looked down on my ignoble self during our initial get-to-know-one-another session).

He was off to a bad start.

"Why did you do it?"

"You waste no time getting to the point. Well... I have really high standards of myself..."

"No offense, but you cannot be serious about having high standards, especially when you tried to commit suicide."

"I was holding in over three months of depression, and that's how it came out. Aren't you supposed to encourage my progress for not attempting it again instead of criticizing me for something that's behind me now?"

"Is it behind you? Or is the real reason related to the constant supervision and monitoring you have been receiving lately? It is almost like being back home, is it not? Pampered like a child. Let me tell you something. You are not really serious about ending your life with a halfway-open bathroom door and your older sister standing six feet away."

"*Step*sister! And are you calling my actions premeditated?"

"I read your file carefully; you are the perfect student. In your mom's eyes, you are still her little girl, the neat and perfect over-achieving angel that would never willingly inflict pain on herself."

"But I did. I indulged selfishly."

"You planned with care and carefully calculated what the end results would be. Fitted everything perfectly to your needs and ulterior motives, and all just so you could draw your mother's attention to yourself. A giant cry for help. I mean, she was obviously too busy with your other two sisters slash sibling rivals, which can be such a scary thing. But there is a reason why she focused on them; they are her husband's children, who she was trying to welcome to the family, especially when one had a drug addiction and the other was not exactly good at picking her suitors."

"Look, maybe to some extent I reviewed my actions before I executed them. But when I found myself on that cold ceramic tile floor, moments before I passed out, I realized my life could be so much more."

"That is the difference between those who do not fear death, and those who are frightened of death and make a half-hearted attempt in order to draw attention to themselves. Even that insight you just mentioned is not authentic because the experience was not genuine."

"Are you accusing me of fabrication?"

"I am. What I need you to understand is there is nothing wrong with the concept of a blended family. And furthermore, your little attention-seeking stunt was not really about your mother, vying for her attention. No, it hardly had anything to do with her. It is silly. You are a charming young woman exuding femininity yet fretting over courtship to an unhealthy degree, resulting in all this mess." His clinician head turned left, then right, disapprovingly.

"Why are you assuming it was over a guy?"

"Well, was it not?"

"Maybe... but considering my own mother knows nothing about my relationship history, I doubt you got this information from my file."

"You are quite right. I got this piece of much-needed-to-be-documented knowledge from the confines of your mind using a quite common technique known as... assumption."

"Assumptions can get you in a lot of trouble, Doc, especially with a Ph.D. plaque on the wall of your office certifying you as a man of clinically-proven methods, not just fortune teller predictions."

"You will have a chance to sue me for malpractice once I release you. Now, tell me what happened."

"That night, he came over... and said a couple of things that hit me really hard. When he left, I fell apart; like completely apart and then..."

"...and then?"

"And then, something happened that's too early to talk about."

"I really think you should talk about this."

"And I respect that, but I am hard-headed and stubborn. So, for someone to penetrate that with a sentence starting with, 'I really think,' is just not going to do it for me."

"Let us try a different approach."

"Let's not. This is something best saved for another time. A time when we have gotten to know one another a bit better..."

"At least tell me if his rejection was the last straw, the incident that pushed you over the edge. Perhaps you are just afraid to admit I am right?"

"You aren't entirely wrong, but you aren't

entirely right either. I need more time, that's all."

Of course, I was severely lying through my teeth. This was it, and he nailed it. There were no additional details, nothing to expound on, nothing else to add, but he was really beginning to agitate me.

And I was not under any oath, nor was this the courtroom scene I had to repeatedly face during my parents' ongoing custody battle, so it was quite all right in my mind that I was being irreverent to God, the good doctor, and the policies at large. He did not have to know any of this, this glorified counselor with his bulky frame, breathing hard and watching me like a hawk with his telescope-lens eyeballs. Not everything I said was inaccurate. He just had to wait and see.

To de-stress, I walked out into the courtyard. The sunlight was brilliant, each ray piercing with warmth. Stealing even a glimpse of the sun caused blotches of discoloration within my eyes, and I had to obliterate the out-bursting heavenly light by closing my eyelids. For the past twenty hours, perhaps twenty-five hours, I realized, I had not been myself, stalling, low on fuel, walking zombified from the track marks on my arms, those prickling violent injections with lengthy needles.

Let us not even mention the pills I had to swallow. But basking in this sunlight, smelling the surrounding vegetation (which only existed in the courtyard), walking up to a tree and breaking off a piece of bark to reveal the sap underneath which I applied like a rehabilitative balsamic ointment to my scarred wrists, made me think; really think.

When I walked back to my room, I realized how spick-and-span everything looked. Everything was so idyllic, missing that daily accumulation of dust. A germaphobe with a dustpan would find neither hide nor hair. The room was spotless, but dust just does not evaporate into non-existence.

At the next conversational therapy session, I brought this to Dr. Murray's attention, "Why was my room searched?"

"I guess they did not do a professional job after all."

"You didn't expect a bunch of amateurs to thoroughly go through a girl's private belongings without leaving a trace, did you? Tell them next time to not leave it tidier than they found it. A dead giveaway!"

"It is interesting you identify yourself as a 'girl' instead of a young woman. Very interesting."

"How about answering my question? I had the courtesy to answer yours."

"I fully expected to get away with it. I did not think you would catch on."

"Takes time to open up; remember that, doctor. Don't delay the progress with missteps like this. I thought your kind had the patience of saints."

"We usually reserve that for the clergymen."

"What were you looking for, anyway? Anything specific?"

"We just wanted to make sure you did not

possess something you could intentionally harm yourself with. That is why we are always watching you."

"You watch me?"

"Are you being facetious, Michelle? You perfectly well know we do. Even when you went for your walk in the courtyard, we were right beside you. Perhaps you did not see us, but I know you sensed us whether you want to admit this or not. You happen to be a very clever girl, Michelle."

"Young woman, Doc."

"That is correct. A young woman who always looks before she takes a step; a step we usually try to anticipate to our best abilities."

"Are all patients privileged to this tasteless treatment? Wait. Why haven't I seen anyone else here?"

"Because there is no one else here, Michelle. This facility is on the brink of being demolished; the land will pass hands to the highest bidder and end up being used for the construction of gleaming condominiums. There is just you and me and many unanswered questions that need filling in." He took a moment to subdue his bursting laughter. "You have a schedule, Michelle. That is why you do not see anyone out in the yard."

"Does everyone?"

"No. They are monitored as a large group with low risk of relapsing. They undergo group therapy and act as sponsors for one another. This reliance on each other is a key component in their rehabilitation process."

"And I am seen as high risk? Potential relapse on the horizon?"

"I hope not, but I do not want to rule it out. It is too early to tell."

"Just great. So, we wait."

"You are in safe hands here, Michelle. Nothing bad will happen to you. A relapse is not always physical, the body's response is just the aftermath which may or may not happen. The idea here is to stop your train of thought once it enters this territory of immeasurable anguish. That is your hideaway from the world where you get to re-enact all your pain up on a stage. You turn into a tragedian."

"Tragedian..."

"This is your safety zone. You isolate yourself there. Playing at being an escapologist, not realizing you cannot escape from a life of disharmony by simply outrunning your problems, locking yourself behind the door of a make-believe world which is just as unbalanced as the one you are trying to leave behind. These delusional fantasies claim so many lost individuals every year, all those poor souls with symptoms not too dissimilar from yours. The deflating confidence, engulfing depression, inability to face reality which unfortunately results in senseless death... in certain extreme cases."

"Thanks for making me feel special, Doc. I'm glad to know there's absolutely nothing different about me. Nothing at all that would make me stand out at the Suicidal Thoughts Convention. Just part of the crowd."

"Michelle, you stand out because you are

alive. You happen to be one of the lucky ones. You have a second lease on life. Be grateful you never fully committed to carrying out what the voices in your head were telling you to do. You tried, but you did not adhere to the rules, follow those rules to the letter. You slit across and not down. Just think, once you are better, you can go back home to your loving parents. Your father's campaign will be over by then, and you can enjoy a little less media attention and settle in."

"How do you know about my stepfather's political career?"

"Why would I not know about it?"

"Because my politically-ambitious stepfather would never allow someone like you—a psychologist treating his suicidal stepdaughter—to have knowledge of his identity. He would use a proxy. Which does tie up a couple of loose ends, doesn't it? This leads me to conclude that you are that proxy, high up on his payroll, that slithering snake, a surrogate for someone else's dirty work, presiding over a simulated sanitorium, and once

the drug regimen makes me pretty much vegeta-
tive, I will continue my stay here indefinitely with
occasional visits from my unenlightened mother.
Just great."

"Michelle, you know this is not true. This
saddens me terribly. You are succumbing to way-
ward thinking bordering on the delusional."

"The theatricality of your gestures, Doc!
We need applause for this riveting performance.
Someone throw a bouquet at this man's feet."

I had caught him with his arm up to the
elbow in the campaign funds cookie jar. He just
sat there speechless and seething, allowing emotions to tongue-tie him in the middle of a mean-
ingful conversation. That was even sloppier than
the job his men did on my room.

Before they brought me here, my mother
visited me in the hospital. It was a brief visit.
The circumstance was morbid, the conversation
forced. She was visibly vulnerable and heartbro-
ken, hardly able to speak, but when she spoke at
last, she alluded to the fact that I was putting a

lot of *unnecessary pressure* on the family, that if one reporter caught wind of a *slip-up* like this, the reportage could cost my stepfather his *entire campaign*.

My stepfather. A man who spent his entire life weighing the odds. He could spot risk a mile away.

I was the high probability risk factor. This place was the deterrent.


For the next couple of days, things returned to normal. Well, almost normal. Outside of the usual-day-to-day routine, I had noticed a change during my regular rounds of depthless conversations with the conniver. Dr. Murray was far more reserved than usual. Less pushy and demanding. A man preoccupied.

Something had changed. I kept imagining a man dynamically descending a set of steep stairs, who suddenly stops. I wanted to know the reason behind this.

I had dislodged something. The truth can be as entrapping as it can be purifying. I looked on with stupefaction, knowing full well that I had hit the nail on the head. And that is when I knew. It *was* just me locked up with Dr. Murray and his strongmen lackeys in this menagerie, watched around the clock by one man (a man watching from the shadows, wrapped securely in his political cloak). Snared, surveilled, and shot on a closed-circuit camera system.

This man. This symbol that refuses to be overthrown.

A man with a brand-new family, a cottage in the Hamptons and a lavish condo on the Upper East Side. Yes, someone who always takes such careful precautions would never allow anyone to publicize his stepdaughter's mental breakdown and attempted suicide in the midst of his crusade for prominence. Not after waging war in the name of his campaign, the battlefield ashen with the charred corpses of his enemies. A man who had always managed any-and-all breaches would

not just stand down or sit around idle and irreso-
lute. All I could do was wait.

More days went by, the typical relentlessness of
time without pause. The installation of a television
set helped, although my allowance only extended
to channels that broadcast updates on my stepfather's campaign.

As much as I hated him, he fought zealously
to the point of almost being the likable under-
dog. That magnetizing snakelike smile greeted me
every single day. I could not escape it. His voice
reverberating inside my head, cuttingly chipping
away at what was once impenetrable. Breaking
me down, making me more malleable. It was all
a little unsettling.

Then came the day I knew it was all over. He was
going to lose the campaign. The public finally saw
through his trickery, and that is also when I knew

it was all over for me. My stepfather was a rabid dog backed into a corner. He had no way out and only one option.

With the current deterioration he was facing, the fickle public with its waning interest, he needed a dramatic turnaround, drastic measures taken to turn the tides of public opinion allowing him to continue his odyssey.

So, I had to die. The showman that he is, I knew he would turn my demise to pure spectacle. Milk it for all it is worth. Want another cliché? He would rise like a phoenix from the ashes to reclaim his spot at the top. A guaranteed victory. I kept probing, trying on other scenarios to see if they fit, teetering between this and that and the other. But I returned every single time. This idea eradicated every other possibility.

After all, here was a savior to a single divorced mother with a teenage child in tow. He opened his arms, he opened his home, he made us a part of his church and hugged us tightly in every photograph. The ideal husband, father, and future leader. The public would see the loss in his face, feel his pain and their own guilt would rise up for betraying him, sleeping with the enemy, favoring his political opponent. At this point he would try to extricate himself from the race until the fickle public would rush back to his side with their bombardment of overwhelming pleas, asking him to stay and not throw in the towel. Sympathy would pour in like a waterfall. The bamboozled public would never turn on him again. And my televised funeral would mark the finale, his coup de grâce. Standing at the podium making a memorable speech, revealing just the right amount of details about my demise, this modest, reserved and much revered public figure would break down just enough to share the cause of the misfortunes that befell his stepdaughter. The maladjustment, slipping grades, skirmishes, substance abuse and attempted suicide, eventually ending up in a treatment facility he paid for until one night she could not handle it anymore and took her own life, shattering the family forever.

And if this was truly his plan all along, the devil's grand design, why the charade with these daily psychiatric sessions, all these painstaking measures taken to mimic an operational facility? Evidence. It had to be that. They were gathering camera footage and documenting my every thought, proof that would support his theories behind my depression and demise. I was unknowingly contributing to my own suicide note. The real note was probably already stashed somewhere for safekeeping, forged in my hand, and written on paper bearing the facility's logo, making it so much more official and final.

This cannot be it... this cannot be how it all ends. I was paranoid. Delusional. It was too absurd. I allowed a smidgen of fear to expand and consume everything. Dr. Murray was here to help. He was here to help me. A clinician with a doctorate's degree. How absurd to think I am alive only because the good doctor thought I still had something important to share.

Around this time, I started to drift off to

sleep, repeating a kind of mantra to myself, *This won't be my resting place...*

As I lay in bed that night (as video-playback would later reveal) Dr. Murray invaded the sanctity of my room. He stood over me for a long time. Watching me. I could not see it from the slightly grainy footage, but I am sure there was a glimmer in his eyes. A horrid glimmer. I have seen it and felt it before. Soulless eyes dispersing infernal light across the vulnerable terrain of my body. Scorching my flesh with his obvious craving. Watching the footage sent shivers down my back.

"It is time, Michelle. I am going to discharge you tonight."

I do not think he cared one way or another if I was awake for what was to come, but I opened my eyes and met his gaze. In the dim light our eyes locked. There was a fixedness in his stare. A steeliness of nerves. He was not preparing himself; he had already reached that stage. His breathing was steady, his voice raspy, like tires skidding on gravel.

"Try not to resist. It will all be over quickly. The more you fight me, the more inclined I will be to use excruciatingly slow and less humane methods. I was about to say try not to scream, or beg for your life, but...

"I guess you could not even if you wanted to with a pillow smothering your face."

He chuckled with no self reproach over his own comment, while I recoiled from his words, unfortunately not fast enough, giving him time to swipe a pillow from under my head and with the debauched swiftness of Marquis De Sade pouncing on his latest conquest, press it firmly over my face.

A methodical killer, he never worried about what he was doing; there was no pivot once he took the first step, and he was pitiless to my pleas as he surely was to all his stifled victims immured to their beds.

"Nothing says affirmation more than asphyxiation," he said as I struggled violently under his strong arms. I needed air, but there was absolutely nothing to gulp at. The air was not there; there was absolutely nothing there.

Just when he overpowered my will to fight and I could not grapple any longer...; just when I was steadfastly becoming immovable; he spoke these words, "I am sure like most people you have wondered at some point about the end. At least now you know."

He kept talking. He would not let me die in peace, serving double duty as an executioner and keynote speaker at my funeral. I relinquished myself to him. He was right. It's not uncommon to wonder how your life will end. And now I knew. I had the golden ticket. The front row seats to a motion picture. I tilted my head back as the parting words to my short-lived life loomed up like credits on that big screen.

But the architecture of that simulated world collapsed, bringing me back, telling me that even a fabricated reality does not last forever, that just like in real life there is no permanence to any-thing; that even the actions of my executioner were transient.

Once the conductor of this torture orchestra reached optimal satisfaction, he slackened his grip on the pillow and I started to lose consciousness, staring uncomprehendingly at his expressionless face.

When I regained awareness, I tasted an acidic res-idue from painkillers I did not recall ingesting. I tried hard to focus my eyes, but the lights in the room were blinding. Here I was coming out of my stupor, pumped full of drugs and still somehow defyingly alive.

Each blink attested to my suspicion of still being inside the "abbey." Yet it did not seem to matter just then, for I felt a seismic sensation against my body like no other. I was part of this kinetic energy, feeling the force of it, the slightest fluctuations of the rippling pattern.

I felt embraced from all sides by a warmth, this soothing balm inducing pleasure and disentangling the knots in my muscles. I surrendered, letting go of all past events, permitting the bathtub I did not quite consciously realize I was in to engulf me.

Then I heard his unmistakable voice.

"You know I look at murder-for-hire jobs with the utmost gravity. Client satisfaction is always at the forefront of how I manage my business, with unprecedented success rates to show for it. Just a few small rules to follow: Never break a contract once accepted and always deliver on time. And it comes with a non-monetary bonus. Torture. Which is apart from the rest and never contractually stipulated by my clients. It is a freebie and as long as I do not leave too many marks everyone wins. Oh, how I do enjoy it. *Tremendously* as you will soon see. I admit some may call it an inner flaw. But I digress."

Dr. Murray became the point of convergence for my now refocused eyes. What I wanted to say was the following, "I call it completely unremarkable. That an individual hired to murder someone might actually enjoy it. It's a pairing concept that has been around since Abel slayed his own brother. And my religious teachings are quite rudimentary, I might add. It doesn't matter how sizable the pleasure is, Doc, it's still a part of the overall equation and therefore your speech is quite typical, been-there-done-that and you will find yourself left behind through the sands of time as some ordinary guy aiding crooked politicians and getting your jollies by torturing your teenage targets. You are not abstruse. Not special or complex in any way. Like I said before, or if I haven't I will say it now: Typical and extremely forgetful." An Academy Award-worthy speech. Unfortunately, no sound waves were detectable. My mouth remained stitched shut. There is a time and place for eloquent speeches. Coming out of a drug-induced sleep, tongue-tied and dealing with cottonmouth could be a strong contender for the most terrible timing imaginable.

Dr. Murray's face remained unchanged; this was a man impervious to awkward pauses in the conversation and he did not care if I replied. His only movement was to moisten his lips with his reptilian tongue. I thought he was gathering his thoughts, using the interim to collect himself before he spoke again, except he never did, never felt the need to continue our conversation since it was the only thing delaying him from whatever it was he wanted to do to me involving this tub, now that he had interpolated me in it and filled it with a warm rejuvenating liquid that made me care-free about whether or not I had the miraculous fortune to live another day. The liquid seduced me with its power, pacifying and assuring me that everything was all right, as long as I stayed sub-merged in it. But now it started to heat up, the water becoming worryingly hot.

Dr. Murray's interest piqued when he noticed my discomfort. He was obviously a man who fervently believed in pain, and he had me right where he wanted me. I was the sole audience to his dissertation on torture techniques. A sad state of affairs for poor little me.

Exercising some of that god-like power, he increased the pressure on the hot water taps. Intolerable pain shot through me. I felt nauseated by the enormity of it. Pain with a sole aim. To triumph. Even through the stupor I pushed, struggled to get out, but Dr Murry's friendly hand on my shoulder kept me down, allowing pain to continue its expansion across my body. To come this far, having faced numerous vicissitudes in my life to end up here being boiled alive.

But not today. I fiercely strived to live, no matter how cruel the world seemed just then, no matter how imbecilic and animalistic were the human actions displayed to me just then, and how mistreated I felt. I found life to be something I wanted, something I desired. I could not allow this pitiless death merchant to blot me out from existence against my will.

The room filled with vapor, with globules of condensation running down the tiled walls next to my head (my only body part jutting above the water) as screams escaped my chimney-like throat. My heart thumped loudly and irregularly; my skin had an epidemic of reddening blisters. And even through all the mistiness, no steam-generated disguise could hide Dr. Murray's sneering expression. This evil creature, this overseer, handler and torturer leering with anticipation for me to die.

And then it happened. My saving grace came in the form of a droplet of sweat which dripped down and made its way into his eyes. I pounced, intercepting this opportunity, disallowing it to slip away while I was still able-bodied to use it.

I pushed Dr. Murray aside, pushed through the overhanging mushroom cloud of steam and made my way out of the room, away from him, away from his homemade torture chamber, leaving a trail of blood in my wake from my still healing wrists which I had reopened with my nails. It was not more than a trickle of blood, but just the right amount to get his attention and lead him straight to me and to my room. But first I had to find my way there through a series of labyrinthine hallways with their seemingly identical levels and doors. Not surprisingly, I never encountered a single soul along the way (more of the good doctor's purported lies exposed).

After some wandering and searching, I finally stumbled across my all-too-familiar containment chamber, ironically happy to be back inside that cell, smiling like a crazed lunatic while darting my eyes all around until I paused on what I had been looking for all along: my bed. I approached it like a madwoman, quickly rearranging the sheets, strategically positioning my pillow, a blanket fort for my personal body double.

I then headed straightaway for the small closet (even smaller since cramping it with my clothes), scavenging and prospecting for weapons.

There I found all that I needed. The cross-piece which I pried from the wall easily enough, and a couple of scarves to patch up my wrists. Lastly, all I had to do was contort my body, bend-ing in half like a gymnast to fit inside, cutting it extremely close as a shaft of light pierced through the darkness of the room.

I watched with bated breath through the narrow slats in the door. The gap widened allowing the intruder to slip inside. He moved around with sufficient care, a sense of purpose. He guided himself across the room noiselessly, always remaining observant of his surroundings, slowly and cautiously working his way toward the pillow placed under the bedsheets. A young girl in hiding.

I solidified my grip on the crosspiece. I was clearheaded, ready to unleash, to pour in all the anger I felt—for my stepfather, this sanatorium, Dr. Murray, and his steamy purgatory.

He removed the blanket and before he could react I braced myself and rushed forward letting out a great bellow, swinging the crosspiece like a baseball bat, trying with all my might to break through the obstruction that was Dr. Murray.

The damage landed squarely on his forehead. I wish I had heard an explosive sound, an excruciating cranial crunch after the hit, one with enough brute force to have left a bloody gaping hole that no staples or stitches or even the best Beverly Hills plastic surgeon specializing in scar revision could ever cure. But I did not have it in me. I was not a murderess. I also was not that strong. So, Dr. Murray, while confused and concussed, was very much alive when I tied him with scarves to the frame of my bed.

Before taking leave of him, I could not restrain myself from giving him a little farewell speech. "You embroil yourself with a high-ranking government official, prostitute yourself for blood money. That's a tough one to extricate yourself from. This man is used to getting what he paid for. He expects results, not colossal failure. There's absolutely no need for me to do anything else here. No need for you to beg for your life. You are as good as dead, Doc. On that note. I think we are done, finished with the treatment, the reforming, I am now going to discharge myself. Goodnight, Dr. Murray. Sleep well."

The rest, my dears, is a happy ending. I not only got away in Dr. Murray's prized possession, his '72 Corvette parked out back, but lived to tell this fascinating tale. The scandalous aftermath was for the news anchors to report, no shortage of sensationalism there. I never did get to sue Dr. Murray for malpractice; he simply vanished. And while there were no bank accounts over-brimming with cash in my real name, or under an assumed identity in Switzerland, I found a decent amount of cash in Dr. Murray's office. Money I was sure came from my stepfather as collateral for a job Dr. Murray accepted and failed to deliver on time which most likely resulted in his death. It was more than enough to get me started on my new journey. Far, far away from here.

# HITCHHIKING WITH...

SOMEHOW, WE MISSED IT. When we eventually became aware of its existence and trajectory it was too late. It shook our deeply-embedded trust in world leaders, the armed forces and the navy, bespectacled scientists, and the astronomers responsible for the President's Aeronautics and Space reports.

It sent people scattering, whimpering, unprepared to deal with such a cataclysmic event. When it hit, its force caused mass destruction, the complete cessation of normality, and relented only slightly in the end, as if acquiring enough conscience to spare a few for preservation of human life on this planet.

Natural selection prevailed, few became fewer, long-standing rivalries resulted in segregation and formation of warring parties, retrogression, collapse of unity, allegiances pledged and further formation of fractious factions giving way to unpardonable imbecility, erratic behavior and irrationality of thought. War enveloped the land, dead covered the soil like scattered grains, everything engulfed in flames, primordial combat depleting natural resources and causing widespread famine; until one day the implacable war, with no resolution in sight, finally ended. Next came a period of catharsis, with the strongest war party issuing a respite to all who joined them. A great proliferation to their numbers, selling dreams, promises, splendorous possibilities, all the while subjugating, brainwashing, clinching the submissiveness of their followers with a non-negotiable contract (the real price of the membership) legally binding them and their offspring(s) for life.

The vanquished non-conformists remained resolute, refusing to join the others (those blind bootlickers incapable of reclaiming their natural rights), deciding to continue living in the old, abandoned cities, enduring intolerable conditions, deprived of manpower and tools necessary for organic progression and forever fugitives in the eyes of those victors who left and went on to form the New World Order. This ruinous state housing the outcasts came to be known as the Human Zone.

Which is where you find yourself, cognizant of the fact you should not be here, knowing well the consequences of capture for anyone illegally crossing into the Human Zone. Especially a reporter with a camera, an apparatus capable of capturing what the New World Order has worked so hard to destroy, the Zone a smear on their painstakingly perfected world.

Their aim is to erase everything that has come before their cherished Utopia. To rewrite history without mentioning the past.

When you were younger, you used to say you were no different from a journalist going out of his way to get to the facts. Now you are one. The right career for someone with a quizzical mindset and a lifelong infatuation with discovering, in the ruins of the past, the book outlining creation itself, a book as old as time itself—the Holy Bible. This obsession with the past is what brings you here today.

Ironically enough, for a desolate place, you encounter someone almost straight away. A single car approaches (a baffling sight, a relic of the past completely restored and in working order). A car! You had wondered how many were still around. Not thinking, as if this is how it should be, sticking out your thumb, you make the car slow down. You ask for a lift. When queried about your destination by the Driver, you reply vaguely, "I wish I knew."

"Get in. You can figure it out along the way." He waits until you get inside before continuing. "You aren't from around here," he says, keeping his eyes studiously forward, such stern concentration seeming excessive to you, considering the solitary vehicle on a deserted road like this.

"That obvious, eh?"

"What brings you out here?"

You look at him, then at the darting landscape through the pristine window of a car long presumed lost to a world that is no more. "Rummaging."

"Is that what you do in the place you come from; you rummage?"

"You could say that. I am a journalist for one of the large corporations. Just out here rummaging for facts."

"The New World Order has all the facts they need. They do not come here. They stay out. Steer clear. Which makes me think you aren't supposed to be here."

"I am not."

"Facts... about...?"

You cannot help but notice a crucifix, gold—now such a worthless metal—hanging from his rear-view mirror. "Our origins."

"Well, son, we are all children of the same father. The Holy Father."

"Opinions may vary."

"What do you mean?" he says and looks at you, clearly the most blasphemous heathen he has ever met in his life.

"Very few people know this place even exists. Call it convenient forgetfulness, a memory lapse, or lack of traditionalist storytelling from person to person, but they never talk about the past, what transpired before. They live their lives in the present with thoughts only about the future."

"But not you."

"No. Not me. I am a logician. A researcher. When the World Leader told me nothing existed before the New World Order came to be, I did not buy it. Mind you, he was really going for it. The hard sell. He was his usual self, personable and undeniably magnetic, I will give him that. Our beloved World Leader really tried to win me over. He even brandished an advance copy of the New World Testament to strengthen his point."

"The what..."

"Revisionist history from the self-appointed World Leader."

"He wrote his own bible?"

"Everyone's forgotten about the Old and the New Testament, blindly wringing their hands before a false prophet fearing jail, public denouncement or worse yet, *beheading* by the leader's own creation, one formerly discovered and named after its inventor, Joseph-Ignace Guillotin."

"This is most unnatural," he says, strangulating the steering wheel with tension-riddled hands.

"What can one expect from a man who crowned himself creator and ruler at his own coronation, placed the crown atop his own head. Since then, he has been burying the past, burying everything that preceded his reign."

"So, he thinks God, or His son Jesus Christ are..."

"A pair of fictional characters. Part of a made-believe world. Not his world. Not his reality."

"And what about you, son, what do you believe?" He turns halfway toward you.

His interest is apparent, and your answer presents some issues as a non-believer. "I am somewhat on the cusp."

"What scares me is not one nonbeliever in Christ, but millions of people who idolize a... a dictator."

"His ambition knows no limits."

"He would be selling his soul to the Devil if he were to go through with the publication."

"The Devil to him is just a minor reoccurring character in what used to be a bestseller."

"If that book is made available to the masses, he will... un-make the world."

"Un-make?"

"A greedy man with an inimical gaze coveting

imperial sovereignty will open the floodgates."

"The flood of Genesis?"

He gestures toward the sky. "The comet was just a warning for what's to come."

"If that were a warning, I would hate to see the imminent hazard we are being warned about. The world cannot handle another disaster."

"You are right, the world would not recover. I repeat, if that book comes out, forget about expiation, expect only the end, the death of the human race. And the suffering will be immense…" He turns to you, and you cannot help but notice the passion in his eyes. "Imagine! One man, mortal human tissue, flesh and blood like you and me, inundating the world with his… his distended ego, his distortions, enacting a false prophet's prophecy attempting to shatter mankind's unbreakable bond; and the people trading devotion to the Lord for idolization of an evil entity simply because they don't know any better. Deprived of the most accurate record of creation—God's very own heavenly blueprints—to reference and guide them in their lives. These same blueprints, which detail the origins of humanity, the birthing of intelligent life with cognitive abilities necessary for greatest possible progression. An account of humanity's preservation, the planting of seeds of knowledge, the ability to construct with basic tools, and using those simple stone implements to build their own world with, tools that sadly turned into weapons with time and innovation, weapons used to commit murder of their fellow men, weapons used to kill the son of God, the child of the master builder, creator of all life on earth. And now your leader wants to hide historical truth from the world, keep hidden the work of God's chosen transcriptionists, scribes in charge of transcribing his miracles with ink on papyrus, preserving the history of humanity's origins. He wants to conceal the truth, hide a book detailing the divine ruler's divine creation. Offering instead a substitution and imposing on mankind his book of falsities as absolute truth."

"Are you a preacher?"

"I used to be, but what I remain is a believer."

Silence shrouded the rest of the ride. Eventually you asked him to pull over. This deserted stretch looked as good a place as any.

A period of pondering and wandering the Human Zone followed until your return to the world on the other side, the progressive world, where you proceeded to wallow in uncertainty until one fated night you decide to act. This was the day before the World Leader was to release his own re-telling of the world.

Disguised, you distribute your unsigned pamphlct solely underground under the title, "Hitchhiking with Jesus." Even after writing, handing out and depleting your stock you remain plagued with doubt. Were you the envoy of Christ, or a mouthpiece for a lunatic? Your words, the story you told, ignited the gunpowder, issuing a challenge to the dictator presiding over a dystopian government. And while you remained uncertain, the people decided for themselves. They spoke the words you wrote. The words you heard uttered in your presence. They chanted these words. They became a form of prayer. The pamphlet became a bible. Words written there seen as scripture. The Warning as punishment for breaking a holy commandment. They reformed their views in accordance to the pamphlet. Pledged to reform their entire lives once they effected a change. But social change like this could only come through blood. Riots broke out, a revolution took place, the World Leader was first dethroned and later assassinated by a member of his close-knit circle of advisers. His book never did see the light of day. All copies were collected and incinerated. There were no more World Leaders for a long while. Oddly enough, you received a promotion, position of restorer of sacred texts, restoring the two editions of the Bible from what scraps of information you could locate hidden in the home of the former World Leader. When you published your efforts that winter, The New World Order seized to exist, officially dismantled, giving rise to new parties and leadership. The mysterious preacher never did say which world would end.

# THE TRAIN RIDE

T HE TRAIN DELAYED, THE STATION teemed with clustered chattering complaining individuals under one roof standing, sitting and pacing impatiently, including insolent businessmen swinging their freshly-polished leather briefcases, blue-collar workers inconvenienced by their over-packed battered valises, and women ranging from professionals to mothers-to-be clutching purses nervously, perhaps as a preventative measure against pillaging by the tricksters and charlatans also gathered there. Those types were also surrounded by the infirm, some wounded and damaged from the war effort, others with tired and defeated spirits and the sadly permanently damaged, mentally defective, heading for the sanatoriums. There one could also find the rising movers and shakers of the business world, missionaries spreading Christianity and the word of God, diplomatic emissaries and emaciated and travel-weary emigres heading to greener pastures. Many resolutely stared ahead. Not all could fit under the station roof and hide from the stifling sun. But they all stood together as a cohesive unit, perspiring terribly in their togetherness on this especially hot windless day.

Nicholas Price was growing slightly impatient himself, checking his wristwatch every so often. Aside from the delayed train and the sweltering sun, a third annoyance had presented itself, in the form of a man partly hidden behind a raised newspaper, one who was clearly observing him.

The looks given were almost imperceptible, completely opposite of incessant. They glided over him, never lingering long enough to become undesirable. The observer did not amateurishly lower the paper excessively or peer over it completely. No, this was someone who knew what he was doing. And he did it well enough, but not perfectly; otherwise Nicholas would have never spotted him.

Whoever the stranger was, he presented no immediate threat. His stare remained open to interpretation. Perhaps it was just a hobby, something the man pursued when he found himself in a crowded place containing a certain person of interest. If it truly were something else, a hidden intent present behind that scrutinizing stare, Nicholas would decisively meet it head on, parry and reciprocate with lethal force.

Nicholas was thirty-five, with a face that was a cold mask, but from time to time his eyes betrayed his humanness. His enemies knew him as an astute, calculating professional with a glacial gaze. They knew him by reputation—the tales about him, his weapon of choice. But they rarely had the chance to look him in the eyes before he pulled the trigger of his Beretta handgun. If they had, they would have seen that fleeting spark of humanity.

At long last, the train noisily approached the platform. Within minutes Nicholas had handed his ticket to the conductor and boarded the train.

Nicholas moved through the slightly claustrophobic carpeted corridor of the train, passed by the prestigious compartments, the substantially larger and fabulously furnished choice of the upper classes, until he located and stopped in front of his own.

Inside he found two benches positioned on the left and the right-hand sides. Above rested, undisturbed for the time being, rectangular-shaped beds that unfolded from the wall— proffering hopefully a night of deep sleep for the weary traveler before being embedded back into their recesses. The ladder was free floating, deployable when needed, and stored in a corner. A single large window with a miniature folding table underneath completed the picture.

Just when he began to get comfortable, sitting down stretching his legs, a stranger invaded his territory, his personal hibernation chamber. The stranger was an unmistakable beauty in her mid-thirties, with not a single thing bland about her physical features. A real head-turner. An enchantress with artistic curves, and wide eyes that engulfed your every ounce of attention, the type you can always count on to make a dramatic entrance, just as she clearly did now. He even found her perfume to his liking, a healing ointment for his tormented soul. "You look like a scorned female in need of emotional healing."

She let out a short, musical laugh. "Do women get any satisfaction hearing you make false assumptions through these stereotypical sexist male remarks, even though after a while they become monotone?"

"I decided against the usual advances of the… quintessential types."

"Sorry, the *what*… types?"

"Quintessential. Representative of a class, in this case of men. Certain types of men."

She raised her thinnest-blade-of-grass thin eyebrows in puzzlement. "So why not just say that?"

"Well you know men…"

"I do?"

"You aren't afraid to talk to me, so you must."

"I'll take your word for it."

"So these men you know, and possibly don't, are notorious for complicating the simplest of things. Case in point, quintessential."

"So these *quintessential* types, are they men of letters, tutoring pupils in educational institutions? Perhaps they are bricklayers who jot down wisdoms about women on tiny strips of paper, pasting them to one side of the brick and passing them down the chain gang, broadening other male minds. Hmm. All these wise men and their collective wisdom! Their wise teachings should be locatable in any public library, cataloged and made available upon request for further study."

"Might take some time to get the funding and permits for a project of this scale."

"And until then, this information is simply out there? Common knowledge spread by word of mouth? Stored in the minds of all men?"

"You don't want to find yourself stranded without a reference."

She sat across from him on the other vacant bench. "Tell me a bit more about these usual suspects and their methods of approach."

He smiled at her self-assured nature. "The approach of a mild-mannered gentleman, for instance."

"Would a mild-mannered gentleman possess enough boldness to even speak to me?"

"He could, in a very mild sort of way…" That disarming smile brushed his face again.

"And the others?"

"Well, the ferocious approach of... let's say wild animals who use brute force, ones that never take no for an answer, the tall tale-tellers, the braggadocio types..."

"I know the type."

"I bet you do. There are far too many of them."

"And where do you fit into the above selection?"

He retrieved a stainless-steel cigarette case from an inside pocket, selecting the second to last cigarette next to the upside down *lucky one*. A vintage lighter lit this luckless cigarette. "My methodology happens to be quite different. Conceit circles around certain men. Especially those impeccably dressed but obviously obscene men with a singular train of thought. Grotesques with grey hearts, bereft of soul and full of ulterior motives. I reference them only as a guide as to what not to do. I have fervor for knowledge, fidelity for seeking out information. I am not rich but neither am I a has-been jabbering incoherencies, one of those constantly down-on-their-luck accursed men. No, I am not like them. I would love to show you just how. Why don't you accompany me to the dining car this evening."

"We jumped ahead, haven't we?"

"Have we?"

"We have. It's what I would call fast-tracking."

"I thought it was just dinner."

"Dinner between strangers is the pursuance of romantic possibilities, but we won't ever get there without you telling me first which category you fit best."

He raised his hands, palms up in mock surrender. "Guiltless. As I said before I am not like those men. I am not sure there *is* a category for me. I get to the point, forgo ornamentation, remain a realist who often walks along the razor's edge. Good at intuiting, full of strong convictions, dependable."

"Dangerous?"

"At times."

"When it's called upon."

"When it's called upon."

"An atypical character, I must say."

"Not your typical chance encounter."

"Hardly."

"Do you approve?"

Her eyes inspected the window, the scurrying sprawled greenery beyond the glass. The whistle sounded as the chugging mechanical beast approached a crossing. "Remains to be seen. I do like the idea of getting straight to the point and skipping falseness, insufferable boredom, the explosive stupefying anger whenever the more swinish type of suitor cannot have their way. My husband was very good at that triplicate."

"*Was.* Deceased?"

"Abandoned. But do spare me the congratulations on my newfound freedom. Do you know why?"

"Because it took such a long time for this annulment to transpire."

"Too long."

"Too long for you to have forgotten who you once were? Outside the abused domesticated housewife who forfeited her rights, her freedom, her previous life."

"It could come back."

"Let's hope sooner than later."

"Why don't we try tonight over that dinner you proposed. See if we can rekindle the fire, even if it is just a flamelet." She gave him a bittersweet smile.

He matched her smile with a more reassuring one. "Accepted."

"I just want you to know he wasn't all bad. I hope I don't sound incurably wrathful about my marriage."

"Don't. I do not like flip-floppers. Nothing you could have done would equal the amount of hurt he inflicted. I could stand here and try to do the same for my younger brother, blame myself, defend his actions, but he was always in control, responsible for himself, for his degenerate ways, his gambling addiction, constantly being in debt with loan sharks and living of all places in Las Vegas."

"Those strike me as different vices."

"Two degenerates sharing one umbrella."

"You don't let go easily, do you?"

"I never let go."

"So, I never stood a chance of declining your dinner invitation in the first place?"

"Even if you had that option, would you want to?"

"I suppose not. Anything is better than the past. Any glimmer of hope. If my father taught me one lesson, that was to always keep my head up whenever something bad happened. To remember that something better would arise as long as I acknowledged the truth. The ability to keep moving forward."

"Now you are on the move."

"We both are."

"You know, it's somewhat of a rarity to have unexpectedly found myself in the presence of a charming..." he paused for a word, found it, "*...coquettish* countess. I suppose I am not a big believer in coincidental meetings, especially aboard a moving train in a cabin I reserved beforehand selfishly all to myself."

"Calling me a *countess* might be an exaggeration. *Charming*, most definitely. *Coquettish* solely depends on the quality and quantity of wine at dinner."

"Sounds divine. I could not have asked for more. A splendid opportunity to spend some quality time with the woman I am going to sleep with..." Nicholas let this phrase linger in the air before uttering its completion, "...in the same compartment."

"Before I fail to recall it at a later date, a friend of yours was leaving you a note under the door while I was inside surveying the premises, having just bribed the conductor to let me occupy it with you for the sheer experience of being in a first-class compartment. Mind you, I didn't get a very good look at him, he kept his face covered with a handkerchief, but he asked me to give you this." She handed Nicholas a folded note.

Inside, written in longhand, were five words: "I KNOW WHO YOU ARE."

Later in the day, our anti-hero and his nameless companion, the charming coquettish countess, traversed along to the dining car, captivated by the guests liberally enjoying themselves.

A whirlpool of activity greeted them there:

The stentorian voices of scurrying waiters, clattering cutlery; scrapping of the constantly moving chairs; patient waiters reminding one of timeless towering Greek statues permanently perched over the shoulders of certain capricious personages vacillating between choices of wine; the constant rotational changing of decimated white tablecloths spotted with insignias of satiety, and everywhere vivacious personalities filling the dining car with resounding laughter.

One sacrilegist decided not to join in the festivities. An oddity. The dullest sort of fellow, one who most likely leads a solitary life, the silent type, detached from the rest of the world, here sitting by himself engrossed in his dinner. A pitiable creature at first sight, with a sallow face and asymmetrical lips.

Nicholas and his dinner guest passed him on the way to their table at the very end of the dining car, close to the wheels, and as such forcing them to lean in closer to be heard.

Once seated and with their order placed, the charming coquettish countess gave Nicholas her best conversation-starter smile. When this subtlety escaped him, she leaned in even closer, taking matters into her own hands, "What should we talk about?"

"What do people generally talk about?"

"They ask questions. Questions that help them leaf through a person."

"To check for suitability?"

"Likeness of mind."

"Suitability."

"Suitability."

"They end up foraging."

"For details."

"To help with their understanding of the other."

"Exactly."

"Exhumation of the human soul."

"Well, it doesn't have to be that deep."

"Doesn't it? Deep conversations are the only ones worth having."

"Why do you find short conversations so unendurable?"

"Because they are short."

"Don't they add up to the same result?"

"But much too late. Some like precision, decisiveness. Some slowness, mundanity. Some can afford to take their time, others can't." His face matched the language, sternness of chosen words.

"It's an issue with time for you then."

"Yes."

"With waiting."

"Very much so. I am not the waiting type."

"That you aren't."

"But some are."

She gave him a hurt look, feeling singled out. "If you are talking about me, I'd say I am somewhat in the middle. I was used to waiting when I was a married woman. I waited for an awfully long time. And then I did not want to wait any longer. But I also did not want to rid myself completely of waiting in my life, so I decided to practice what you could call the fifty-fifty principle."

"I didn't mean you, just so you know."

She exhaled with relief. "Oh. I thought you did mean me."

"No, no. I meant the gentleman sitting two tables up from us. Medium height, far from lustrous hair, receding in fact, unshaven, slightly overweight if there ever is such a thing as slight. His clothes are up-to-date, modern, fashionable, but wrinkled. His dinner is entirely predictable, bland."

She turned her head a little, shifted her eyes to the gentleman. "You really have him pegged.

I appreciate how you dismantled him using your power of observation, I just don't understand why."

"It's simple. His actions are premeditative. He wants us to think he's having a straight-forward dinner, sitting alone minding his own business."

"But he isn't."

"No. He certainly isn't."

She paused. "What is he doing then?"

"He is observing. Listening."

"I don't see the big deal. He is alone. He is lonely. So what if he looks around a bit?"

"He's looked in only one direction with any real interest, aside from his feigned interest in his dinner. In ours. At us."

"Well so much for a conventional conversation."

"Predictability pervades most conversations. Aren't you tired of predictability?"

"Well put. I suppose I am."

"One must strive to be uninhibited, anomalous,

completely original in the presence of someone as lovely as you." She blushed, darting her sparkling eyes downward. "You are good." She paused, slightly uncomfortable. "That man wasn't really watching us, was he?"

"No, of course not. Just me. But do not worry, he is most likely a poorly miser with miserly fixations such as voyeurism. He likes to drop in on other people's good time. Let him get an eyeful."

"And an earful."


In their shared compartment, Nicholas watched the woman sleep. Complaining of migraine pain, she retired early, swallowed a capsule and closed her eyelids, waiting for the calmative effect to take place, not wanting to face any more reality.

He had felt tired as well, and favored the idea of joining her in hibernation. But now he was having too much trouble falling asleep, tossing and turning in his bed.

Over the course of his lifetime, Nicholas had

never considered himself lucky or blessed with remarkable gifts. His skills were painstakingly accumulated, chiseled in solitary practice as part of his ascetic lifestyle, unaided by others whose teachings he abhorred. He abstained from the usualness of things, fully entrusting himself to the doctrine of self-reliance and perfecting those skills over many years.

The one noteworthy advantage he had over others was his acute hearing. But this was both a blessing and curse, as his ears were hellbent on picking up everything, constantly alerting him, bringing to the forefront even the most meritless noises.

After an hour of trying to sleep, Nicholas, no longer even groggy, sat up in bed. His eyes spun about the room, scrutinizing, probing, until he found himself focusing on the cabin's door. He strained his eyes, refocused his vision. Something on the other side was blocking the streak of light between the door and the floor. The width of the intruder's shadow suggested a single person.

And while the strange figure had not intruded, he was probably intending to, poised and listening, waiting for the right moment to strike. Nicholas reached under his pillow and retrieved his loaded, suppressed Beretta—the safety already off so as not to make any noise. Some would call this rush dizzying. But for him, there was only a feeling akin to oceanic calmness. This was second nature. Nicholas tightened his grip on the handle, the gun an open invitation for the intruder to step inside.

However, the knock announcing this lurker's presence never sounded. The door handle never turned. A lockpick never got inserted to manipulate the lock. Was it timidity? Hesitancy? Second thoughts? Even over the clatter of the train, Nicholas heard a distinct rustling as another poison pen letter slid underneath the door. More insinuations, character defamation, perhaps a request for the almighty dollar.

The real truth was certainly ascertainable. Nicholas firmly believed in logical deduction, the discoverable nature of even the most complex problems. There was a perfectly sound justification for this interloper's actions, the driving force, the motivational factor behind their criss-crossing paths aboard this train. Nicholas would figure it all out in his spare time once he did away with the burdensome aspect of the murder.

He moved quickly, quietly unlocking and opening the door, cautiously stepping over the note on the floor, just in time to catch sight of the fleeing quarry. The straight-line layout of the passenger car certainly simplified matters. Nicholas smiled, a secret smile implying a private joke: in his need to flee, the stranger forgot the cardinal rule of reconnaissance—look behind you. Except for prey and predator, as Nicholas dubbed them in his mind, the corridor was empty. The stranger carelessly kept propelling forward, traversing the tight passageway, still never bothering to look back, aiming for the connecting doors between the cars. With his sole focus forward and zero visibility behind, the stranger made for an easy target.

Nicholas picked up pace, moving in for the kill.

He shortened the distance, positioning himself directly behind his oblivious victim fully immersed with the task at hand of trying to open the connecting door.

Nicholas pounced, smothering the man's mouth, not wanting to hear any exhortations for life, then raised his gun, tightly gripped by his other hand, and struck down hard, liberating his victim of his consciousness before promptly extracting the stranger's limp body back with him, averting any suspicion along the way through pretense: A pair of boozed comrades supporting one another with linked arms, both returning to their respective cabins.

He kept up the charade until he reached his compartment. Straining slightly, supporting the stranger's weight, he opened the door, noting satisfactorily nothing had changed in his absence. The compartment remained the epicenter of dead silence, with no detectable stirrings.

Nicholas lowered the body, dragged it inside far enough to clear it of the door's path, then closed the door gingerly with his outstretched foot. His eyes never left the sleeping beauty's face in her berth as the lock *clicked* into place. He waited but did not spot any facial twitching or notice any changes in her breathing.

This made him smile, having dodged the undesirable. Nicholas took hold of the stranger once more, dragging his unconscious body toward the window, a short distance in very tight quarters, until his heel bumped against a solid surface, feeling the materialized back wall with one hand.

Nicholas stood up at full height. A momentary pause. The much-needed break from all the physical effort. He stood there, motionless except for his eyes. Eyes that roamed. Eyes that moved along the compartment until they met another set, the woman's, now widely opened, full of alertness.

She slowly sat up, reaching for her glasses. The situation clearly was an ungraspable one for her.

Nicholas gripped her unsteady hand, stopping her from putting on her glasses. He manipulated her arm downward, setting it on her lap, met there eagerly by her other slightly trembling hand—now an even set of two, trembling together, positioned in a payer position around her spectacles. Nicholas then placed his palm over her eyes, gently shutting her eyelids.

Through the crevices formed by his splayed fingers, she fought hard to focus, fought against her farsighted vision, battling the blurriness, and briefly improving the distortion enough to witness the veil of darkness suddenly lifted, and the compartment filled with a bright torchlight flame.

Unmistakable to a woman whose husband hunted as a pastime, her ears knew the ever-eerie sound of the bullet leaving the chamber, quelled by the silencer. About the same time, she smelled the rush of hot air that resembled sulfur.

While many would have taken a look just

then to satisfy their curiosity, their inquiry confirming or denying the conclusions arrived at, she saw this as a terrible mistake which would only lead to certain death.

Her death.

So, she remained still, remained seated, statuesque, even with Nicholas bustling about her. She could not pinpoint his every movement, but she could tell he had his hands full moving around the compartment altogether unsuitable for three people. That is why she supposed he was removing the third party...

She felt nauseous inside, holding back a hysteric outburst, her organs squirming and refusing to stay put. A living being, breathing the same air, cut down mere seconds ago...

Slight noises reached her, and then a breeze that started to sanitize the stagnant, sulfuric air. Nicholas had opened the window. How else would one get rid of a body in here? This moving cramped catacomb. He was now bent over the body, lifting it, the dead dangling arms reminding her of a drowned man fished from a river. And out that body went, discarded like refuse, scattered from the window like ashes—abandoned to decay in the wilderness.

She could not help to wonder about the view outside. Her thoughts, unfortunately, could not reach a consensus. In one version she saw the clear window, outside of which farmland greeted her, constant and uneventful. The houses looked similar, with rotting wood, peeling paint, barns housing farm stock, blossoming flowers, and an overall prolonged stillness except for the lightly wavering grass.

In the second version, the blood spatter has smudged the window. Outside, the land is barren, with something under the surface giving it movement, a bubbling beneath causing earthly tremors, draining and unnerving her, peeling and stripping away, a concocted nightmare cannibalizing her, trying to satiate its appetite for succulent humanity.

After he disposed of the body, he came over

and held her under a wool woven blanket. His touch was oppressive and singeing to her skin. Her mind raced feverishly.

Nicholas awoke to the feeling that something was not how it should have been. The scene, his present reality modified, his design tempered with. Sunlight spilt through the window and the blanket lay flat against the bed. The train had stopped, and he was all alone. An occurrence he had not anticipated had taken place in the middle of the night while he watchfully kept his eye on her resting body.

He must have closed his eyes, entering deep sleep, dreaming for once, an absurdist dream ripped right from the pages of a fantasist's notebook. In the dream Nicholas was choking the murdered man. The man kept rasping, gulping for air, trying to express himself in a garbled language, a communication system consisting entirely of guttural noises a gutted animal might make.

Her disappearance was unmistakably a hindrance. He had to attend to the situation immediately, and he was already behind. Losing time where it counts most always puts you in an inferior position. But he would find her and make her understand. Persuade her with pleasant words or deaden the hollow pain she must feel inside right now; the type of pain that circulates continuously while always returning to the heart to inflict more hurt.

Nicholas holstered his gun, left the cabin and with great concentration descended the locomotive to the brightly-lit sidewalk, slightly past the train station. The train must have just perched here, the screeching halt intrusively cutting through the fabric of his slumber. Thankfully this happened to be the penultimate stop before his own.

He head-hunted for her along the paved paths illuminated by the sun's brilliance, until he collided with a current of people, all in a rush, blurred faces in fast-motion heading toward their different destinations. He marvelled at the militant synchronicity of their steps. Disoriented now, unsure of his destination, fearing this marching battalion might single him out, he infused himself with them, surrendering himself to the mob, not wanting to be the one who stopped.

Once he synchronized himself, figured out the rhythm of the crowd, he moved with gracefulness. His gaze passed over concrete businesses, and brick residential homes, moving and parked cars, signs signaling direction and enforcing rules, more moving and stationary foot traffic, and air polluting trucks and buses all crammed into one area of a busy bustling city. And just when surrender seemed imminent, he found himself staring at a picturesque sight, one he nearly missed:

A park filled with devotees to the sun, a divine and paradisiacal place, full of blossoming flowers and immeasurable greenery trampled underneath the feet of happily screaming children chasing one another and passing the bench where she sat deep in thought.

She stared ahead with unbroken concentration, the sun's curative properties wholly lost on her. With a furrowed forehead and a face reflecting nothing but fear and worry, she emitted none of her usual radiance. She was alone on the bench, as if all the others were keeping a certain distance, sensing her wanting to be alone.

Nichols sat down next to her. She never acknowledged him, kept staring hypnotically ahead. He looked around, remaining calm and estimating the value or risks.

They happened to be in a very popular part of the park. The situation did not greatly improve when Nicholas noticed two constables speaking in the dialect of the region, positioned some distance away, but a bit too close for comfort.

"You are distraught, that's understandable. Don't you think I understand? I am wholeheartedly on your side."

"You are bereft of conscience."

"You think less of me now?"

A look of incredulity passed over her face.

"You murdered a man."

He eyed the constables, said nothing.

"And for what?" she said. "Why?"

"Self preservation. As absurd as this notion is, I was not willing to forfeit my own life. I could sit here and attempt to justify my actions, attempt to lessen the impact. But we both know I won't."

Her hand whitely clenched the edge of the bench. "Are you going to murder me now?"

"I don't have to. Mum's the word, right?"

"How can I live with myself?"

"The same way you lived with yourself when you became stuck in a loveless marriage. Bear through it. That's all any strong woman can do."

"Did you actually feel nothing? Not an ounce of pity? You could have spared him. Tied him up. He wasn't a threat to you then, lying on the floor comatose, defenseless."

He looked over, looked away. "It's almost impossible to stop once you start."

"But you didn't even try."

A quick nod. "That I did not."

"You know... I think you did feel something. You felt empowerment, releasing all that hatred you felt as a child—jealousy, parental love distributed unequally between you and your brother. Acceptance cannot be gained with a pistol, and neither can love."

"Freudian assumptions aside, my childhood was a happy one. Swell. Uneventful."

"And yet look at you now... A journeying Satan."

"And here I thought you might refer to my voyage as a spiritual pilgrimage!"

"More like the path of a disease. Pestilence dead set on wiping out humanity."

He snickered. "Such archaic concepts. Biblical. Reeks of righteousness. Sadly, it just doesn't work in this rotting world that has disowned all higher power."

"Have you noticed, that as much as you try to anticipate your opponent's next move, they still once in a while find a way to surprise you?"

"I wouldn't do that if I were you. I would not have given it thought to begin with, but now that you clearly have, make sure you do everything in your power not to give it another. As much as I have enjoyed our conversational interlude, I want to remind you that I do not feel languid, nor have my body or mind atrophied sitting on this bench. And you would be greatly mistaken if you think I have not spotted those constables to our right, entranced in a very lively conversation, it seems. Whatever is being discussed, it must be utterly enthralling for these two public servants to have completely forgotten about patrolling, completely forgotten about being the watchmen of the street and that in their absence, or in absence of their complete attention, there might be a rise in all sorts of criminal activities, a direct correlation if you will. Preoccupation with a subject is great; complete immersion is extremely dangerous."

"How did you describe yourself when we first met? Dangerous at times, if I remember correctly. Isn't that so? Perhaps so am I. Perhaps I should get up and stretch my legs."

"I do believe this would be a fatal mistake. A clear case of threadbare logic."

She turned to him, fully facing him, smiling crazily at her potential executioner. "So, you *are* going to kill me."

"If you force my hand."

"I wouldn't be able to live with myself if I didn't try to stop you."

"Ah, that prickling sense of duty. The need to right a wrong and administer justice. To rush to those two constables and pronounce distinctly, without delay, that right behind you sitting on this very bench is the scourge of society—a man who murders. And who could blame you? You are blameless. These emotions are not counterfeit. You have an obligation. To yourself. The world at large. The society you are a part of. It all has that ring of trueness to it. Hell, it's downright inspirational really, I'll give you that." He shrugged. "The sad reality is that you wouldn't even have the time to stand up."

"Do you think that scares me?"

"It should. But I know it does not. Not when it's just you and your sense of justice."

"You know me well."

"I do. I even know things that you tried to keep away from me. For example, do you know what the word 'anthesis' means? It's of Greek origin, roughly defined as, 'to blossom,' which is something your unborn child cannot do, blossom that is, if it's short-life is further shortened by an irretrievably bad decision made by its law-abiding mother."

She let out an unnatural fit of laughter, momentarily drawing the attention of the two constables.

"I will only warn you once more. There will not be any warnings after that." Nicholas slid his hand inside his jacket pretending to search for something in the breast pocket, unholstered his gun and hid it amid a great many pages of a discarded newspaper next to him. "When I think about the first time we met, what stood out for me the most was your smell. I could really smell your perfume, the fragrance of perspiration left behind on the back of your neck, and, of course, the fragrant smell of your unborn child. We have my increased nasal sensitivity to thank for a more level playing field. It seems we both have something important to lose. I just hope you make the right decision."

If I may interject, this remarkable story will not have a conventional ending. The ending splinters into a pair of distinct possibilities:

In his version, Nicholas succeeds in convincing her. A truly triumphant moment. He has no doubts about her ability to keep a secret. He has made his point, and she has understood everything. She even agrees with him, admitting she was rash and over-zealous in her pursuance of justice.

He watches the children playing, digging trenches in the sandbox. Allying themselves against a common enemy. The enemy is unseen, but its presence is felt and they continue to dig at a more frenetic pace, fortifying their position. These are not your ordinary children, this is a unit, each member persnickety about completion of their assigned task. Their insularity on full display. Neutralization of the foreign enemy to ensure their country's survival. Their structure would not crumble, the unit would not cower. This trench would be a resting place to some of them, those whose prayers will go unanswered. The dignified death of a true soldier. A befitting death. The big one might have been over and forgotten by the world, but these smaller and equally personal wars were still being waged.

Nicholas extricates himself before the first shot rings out, the air thick with threat. They are surrounded from all sides. He knows the outcome facing those soldiers, those condemned men with darting, sunken eyes.

His own eyes dart, as if anticipating something. Seconds later, a car—elegant, enormous, colored black after a tar explosion—comes to a halt and stations itself near the exit to the park.

Nicholas stands, commemorates their chance encounter with a firmly planted kiss on the lips, and enters the automobile's familiar leather-bound interior with ease. His occupancy reanimates the vehicle, tailpipe discharges wrath as the passenger side window slowly rolls down. It is absurd to see the sarcastic, almost sneering smile, to hear his undignified laugh, but it is there in the richness of his handsome, unaffected face. The window rolls back up, the automobile flies forward and disappears.

In her version: She stood up.

# THE LAST LAUGH

I AM JUST GOING TO SAY THIS: rejection is tough to accept, tough to swallow, tougher still on unaccomplished rising stars, tough even on the toughest professionals, the risen stars, the accredited accomplished performers of stand-up comedy who to this day may still experience the occasional heckling, or booing, and feel rejection's venomous sting. No amount of preparation truly prepares you; no amount of bracing improves upon the impact of that prickling sensation. You do not get to walk away unscathed; be thankful you even get to walk away, unlike some of those greener newcomers.

The barbarianism of The Audience, an audience that can talk back. Have a voice of their own, even though they are not the ones up on stage holding the microphone. The pomposity of the enthroned performer. The delusional thought processes of the artistic mind. Thinking he can evade the menacing eyes, escape the mounting tension of expectation, standards set skyscraper high in that opulent room. Wanting to prove them wrong, win them over, conquer and convert those witnesses to his highs and lows. Laughter, the lifeblood of any comedian. Attainment of praise. Receiving tabloidal recognition. A cushioned performance. A great success! Menacing faces unmasked, the room flooding with humanness, projecting back reassurances to the comedian on stage, knowing now with certainty that he has converted them, that they are his, their deafening applause is for him, that it all belongs to him from now on, the clapping, the cheering, the admiration, idealization, his kind of crowd, avowing to follow him, the comedic Messiah to the very end, to his final farewell performance.

And this is exactly how it was for the longest time until the slippage. Then came the rejection. The tough to accept rejection. Even tougher without a proper explanation. Like a lover departing without so much as leaving a farewell note. Deafening silence replaced the applause. Lackluster attendance followed. The Audience even lacked energy needed for the usually charged heckling and booing. They just got up from their seats and left the room. The venues changed; opulence replaced with decrepitude. Soon the appointment book was wide open, unimpeded with scheduled or unscheduled performances. I retreated to my condominium; security afforded through amassment of funds from previous more successful shows. Confined to a catacomb, none the wiser as to the reason. It bothered me. The reason. Engulfed in the unknown. Harboring resentment at the lack of clarity, forever living with the remembrance of those unmuzzled barbarians letting me know exactly what they think. Unable to forget the sensation of dampness, my clothes drenched, doused in their critique. Unfortunately, not a very in-depth critique since I never did learn the reasoning behind their rebellion. Simply capitulating to their demands, the demands of the audience, signing the contract signaling my immediate retirement from the stage, from holding the microphone with a firm grip. Betraying my artistic roots. And once I finished and put down the pen, they did not so much as offer a thank you. No commiseration from that mob. It is as if this is exactly how it should have been all along. The beckoning hand of the butchers, ready to slaughter you. One guillotine reserved for the unamusing comedian.

This sanction, this sacking of my long-built career, can hardly be considered an inconsequential event. It is anything but that. A dreadful development. A magnitudinous setback. Living a meaningless existence, grievous over what once was. In the absence of a career, that feeling of excitation disappears. Everything joyous disappears. What remains is the horrible immensity of time on one's hands. To live with oneself. Split responsibilities of performer and spectator. Most unnatural to a comedian, a performer, accustomed to being projected onto the lives of others. And I know what you are going to say, so spare me. Pain takes time to heal. Don't I know it. Don't we all know it? The problem is, when there is just so much of it, you begin putting up fences, boarding yourself up from the rest of the world while wallowing in severe depression, trying to reach out to others for help while not coming to terms with the real issue. Acceptance of the current reality as the only real way of stopping the cycle of self abuse. The hinderance of heightened emotionalism. Depleted, I felt revulsion toward the world at large, nothing to rouse me from this torpor. I committed the worst sin known to a performance artist. I slowed down. Even unwanted, I could have kept creating, kept writing, each joke repudiating their ruling. Instead I entered this paralytic state, lodging there, registered as a dissuaded artist/ dead artist in the reservation logbook. Having done about the worst thing a person can do to themselves. And I remained there, waiting. But waiting for what?

In this concocted state I bereaved my career, too incurably embittered to see some semblance of light at the end of the dark tunnel. Some glimmer of hope. A cavernous hole formed deep inside my chest. Compelled to close this opening, I resolved to using food, a poor substitute in hindsight, as a stand-in for bricks to cover the passage. Patching this hole did not expunge the void accompanying me wherever I went. In an almost masochistic fashion, in the course of time, I stopped worrying; I became enthralled, captivated with this chosen for me calamitous path. I went along, barred myself from the outside world living inside of my monastic retreat. Revelling in my reckless pursuit, consuming mammoth portions of comestibles. A guttural gluttony of everything under the sun. A complete wipeout trying desperately as a last resort to lessen the internalized pain, trying to escape the inescapable memories of uncongested rooms, unobliging audience, stationary hands of the unenthused crowd refusing vigorous clapping, refusing a standing ovation.

Excessive weight-gain followed. What did I expect from a stultified stationary existence spent in a swivel chair? Combine this with the refrigerator and all its unprotected provisions so close, just a few push-offs away, and you have a disaster in the making, the steaming cauldron, the Witches' Brew from Macbeth. What started out as a harmless pastime naturally progressed to something more sinister, spiralling out of my control, innumerable insatiable intakes, administering everything I could get my hands on down my esophagus, simply unmanageable by someone who lacked self-control, was weak-willed, with arms that should have been straight-jacketed.

I was constantly a victim to this animalistic hunger, these rippling pangs, this insufferable ravenousness, always there, always looming above, encircling from all sides, triggering, provoking, driving me into a corner where I crouched, curled up, defeated and completely powerless. This weight gain, this excessive blubber, came to define me. Not so much a rough patch, more like my life in a nutshell. It took some time to accept this fact, that when I go to bed, I am not going to wake up in the morning any skinnier, maybe even bigger, making that weight scale needle climb higher and higher until it has no place to go.

This predisposition to weight fluctuations always existed, a regrettable inheritance courtesy of my parents. I rallied and fought hard against it in my younger years. The formative years. The only fighter in my family, really. But once I reached some level of cognizance, all hope withered away. With this newfound clarity I started to understand the root problem with my family, the true underlying causes behind my weight gain outside the diminished MC4R gene, the fact that no one in it had any heart or a soul. My father tuned everything anyone said to a low frequency his old police scanner would not even pick up. A once great man, retired from the force after more than thirty years of service, helping people left and right. But at home, he could not even listen to his own children or wife's demands. My mother, on the other hand, had a nasty habit of getting behind the wheel of our old beat-up van and driving away whenever emotions struck her. An unfulfilled woman, constantly enervated, easily spooked, unequipped to deal with high intensity situations, like the daily squabbles between her and her husband, she tried to salvage what she could of herself, what parts remained, and in this she would find no opposition from anyone else, this was hers and hers alone. Hardly an idyllic household. Intermittent tremors rattled the foundation, caused by unsticking of once deadlocked familial bonds, shaking the established stronghold housing two adults and four children. It is always fascinating to return, to leaf through that old family album, to elucidate your childhood experiences from a more mature perspective, provide commentary with insights to painful events eluded in childhood.

It is not surprising I turned out how I did. A damaged outcast who thought for a long time that his life was not going anywhere.

I do apologize, dear reader; I do not mean to sound self-dramatizing. But I do think there is plenty to scrutinize in our past, the precursor to countless individuals' defective maturation, stunting the growth, causing irreparable damage to the mind. Specialists cite improper handling from the very beginning, mishandling of the young impressionable mind. Very much like my own at the time of my testimony. So please, allow me to continue, to bring you to my level, where you will gain knowledge and understanding as to the function and purpose of each individual cog in the mechanism, the inner-workings of me. Allow me to unburden myself.

As I was saying, these people, this so-called family, flattened my expectations. The effects are still present, still settling like dust in a recently vacuumed room. A reminder of pain's immortality. Pain that still wanted very much to undermine, ambush, breach the fortified fort I relentlessly spent so much time strengthening, hoping it would prove resilient during subsequent attacks. Pain that remained. Engaged in a never-ending assailment. Storming the fort, with me constantly repairing the damage to the walls.

I can still recall the inconsiderable favoritism. Only choosing to love those they understood, those whose emotional problems they could solve easily. Never for a moment contemplating the damaging effects bestowed upon the youngest child through these tactics. The seldom care, something that should have been a birthright. My siblings were the true beneficiaries, while I faced unremitting besiegement.

Time passed, my parents held on to their ways, unable to relinquish, remaining incorrigible, no room left in their lives for ideas about self-betterment and generally better parenting. These were older people, set in their ways, non-conformist and non-pliant. Custodians from the underworld, and I the sacrificial lamb. My mother began disappearing more and more frequently, trying to locate a haven for her drinking problem and compensate for the love she was not getting at home with strangers she met on the wide-open road (or the parking lot of the nearest bar). My father, the heavily inebriated bum, mostly watched telly, guzzling down the contents of the "next" can of beer without so much as a comment, nervously running his hand through his thinning hair and only getting up to stumble to the bathroom, usually leaving behind a sprinkling of scaly skin on the floor. He never lost his grip on the drink; it was his mind eventually checking out on a leave of absence that caused him to become incommunicado for days at a time, trading his insignia of ill-humor for psychopathic lashing-out, usually with a belt, buckle side to buttocks, back and sometimes face. A tuned-out tyrant terrorizing his own helpless child, unresponsive to any number of imploring pleas and nightmarish screams.

I spent most of my adolescent life wishing I were dead, so all the pain collected over the years would go away, and I would not have to wake up and face a living hell. This is around the time my eating disorder developed, not that anyone in my family bothered to notice that anything was wrong with me.

Then came the suicide attempt that got everyone's attention, my fifteen minutes of fame with my own family, although even then, they did not say much about it, unable to comfort, to express, to feign care beyond shock and surprise. To draw from a tank with an insufficient supply of emotional empathy. Foreigners to my feelings. I take that back. One family member did have something to say. My oldest sister Sandra said, "I guess I have to call poison control now," after discovering me spread out on a bathroom floor, having washed down Tylenol with carpet cleaner. It was her boyfriend's birthday too, so she was especially angry with me. I do not remember much except the emergency room, the one therapy session, being discharged and being prescribed anti-depressants, which I thought I would be taking for the duration of this life and the next.

The saving grace of the matter was not having to worry about how my parents felt. Apathetic, sighing, pronouncing this as mere acting out, sweeping it speedily under the rug. No attempts made to deal with their fear-stricken child. Emotional responsiveness would not be prised from these people. A pair of warped characters, perceiving suicide as a trivial matter, alumnus and alumna of the old school teachings: some things are better left unsaid. Talking perceived as a sure sign of weakness, especially with the least liked family member, inviting vulnerability, surrenderment of self to verbal communication with a nauseating nuisance, a misbehaving little vulgarian.

How I craved the naturalness of normalcy, a

normative family dynamic. To nab the spotlight occasionally. To have a chance to stray from my permanent state of quietude. Engage in conversations, practice communication, have a proper outlet for my self-expression. I had a whirlpool of opinions. Unfortunately, all brushed aside. I felt like I did not exist at all. When hatred replaces love, it can be a stimulant that motivates you to succeed in the eyes of those who want your downfall.

Since my declarative gesture went unnoticed, unable to reassert my presence, remind them of my existence, convince them of our connectivity, all those failed attempts, I decided to renounce them, end the cycle of abuse, reconstitute my life, a fresh start, follow in my mother's footsteps and salvage something, hopeful the rescued piece proved sizeable enough to help me build upon and guarantee anything other than placement on a dirty stool of the local watering hole, dismantling my stress through drink, downturned lips realigning themselves to a would-be smile just to take the next poisonous sip, then returning to the previous state, unofficially undertaking the role of a describer of all faults with the world, desperately trying to convince anyone who would listen how terminal life is.

I wanted hope. A hope for the future. So, I moved out. There were no exaggerated theatrical partings, no severance of speaking terms for they did not exist, just a forfeiture of family ties for a clean slate. I packed my life away in a few duffle bags and left. This perfectly-timed escape emboldened me to tackle the world. Speculative prospecting followed, dead-end jobs, rental struggles, until sometime later, down the road of maturation and encountered disappointments, I decided I wanted to become a comedian. Cheaper than any therapist, and what better profession to channel your anger and still receive a steady paycheck. A chance to be the center of attention, lights flooding the stage, a packed venue, all eyes on one man with a microphone, a humorist parading in front of them; the live audience, an entertainer purposely acting like a poppycock, a medieval period court jester time-travelled to a modern-day comedy club. Sure, it might seem contrived, automated, writing and telling jokes to benefit others, needing their approval, their rating, but eventually you get to take the reins and do for "self" what you have been doing for "others." And this starts with a single moment. You will know when it comes. That pivotal moment, the big win, a moment of pure artistry, incremental changes beginning to take place from one home-run-landed joke, so paramount to a comedian's success, a stroke of luck when your painstakingly prepared material wins them over. You start seeing a suffusion of smiles, bustling about originating from pure excitement, pure magic, opening of barricaded doors, dissolvement of the barrier between performer and the audience, you gain ability to cross over becoming one of them, nested, chosen, part of a family you never had. You gain the ability to write for yourself, please yourself foremost, while still being swarmed by adoring fans. I was meant to play this role. And play it perfectly. I was a natural. It all came so easily. Almost second nature. I suppose it helped to grow up surrounded by unswayable Neanderthals, disheartened and hostile, impossible to please. The dysfunctional household where I planted the seeds for future career harvest. A practice run for the toughest-to-please club audiences on my comedic pilgrimage.

And when they stop laughing at your jokes? Is that what you are asking, dear reader? Well, you know all about that already. Which brings us right around again, back to the present. The inescapable present. Where I find myself reading an invitation to perform in the party room of my condominium. A thirty-minute set. First gig, first opportunity in almost three years. A rupture in the routine, weaning from mundaneness. Summonses of success. That fleeting second chance up for grabs. A precious opportunity for career resurrection. No, an advantageous opportunity for a confrontation, the jilted lover accosting their former romantic partner, accruing insight, enlightenment, an explanation for the change of heart. Although, I instantly foresee a problem. With my niche interest in ingestion of food, immense amounts of it, I have gained considerable poundage; instead of having far-flung interests, I zeroed in, focusing obsessively until I found myself in a perilous state, worshipping a temptress, and as a long-term tenant in her temple, I would have to break the lease.

I cringed at the idea, simultaneously noticing my shirt had a covering of crumbs, in addition to being decorated with patterns of sweat embroidery. I could feel them now, sweat rivulets lubricating my useless limbs, nailed to my swivel chair, itching terribly, thinking about this uncooperative body of mine. I had to start reshaping my thought patterns, and I was more than willing to tackle the toilsome task of standing up for the carrot-invitation dangling before me, although, the actuality of implementing my thoughts within the realm of reality was a bit more difficult, to move those immobile feet, tear through that tremendous enjoyment those feet felt of true inactivity, feet with slight archness to them enjoying surface comfortability of a wool-silk blend of a great Persian carpet.

Yes, a true natural at wasting time, completely in my element. My body a blunt tool, a symbol opposing optimal fitness, my mouth when not occupied with large quantities of food issuing declarative statements, protestations against progressive pedestrians with quick nimble feet and ability to keep a steady pace. Enough! Enough idling. I looked above, greeted at once by the sturdy metallic handle suspended overhead, lonesome and anticipating the reaching hand, a handle attached to a length of galvanized wire rope attached in-turn to a set of heavy-duty wheels on a ceiling mounted movable track tracing the interior of the condominium, not at all dissimilar to a pulley system, albeit reconfigured, improved upon and able to hold upwards of four hundred pounds.

I fastened my fingers around the handle, getting on with the programme. I tugged mightily; it held; a system holding strong, manufacturer's promise upheld, a system working exactly as it should, a dependable continuous source of support reassuring me I had not exceeded the weight limit. Wheezing, I launched myself to a standing position. Severest punishment to my body. It is noteworthy to say that my task seemed a tad bit easier imagined than the implementation at hand now: a treacherous journey beyond the kitchen and the stainless-steel refrigerator. I blinked, took a step, then another, a sequence of footsteps, beginnings of acceleration, footsteps thundering, floorboards creaking, my eyes watering. I looked down at my shirt, it looked ridiculous, crumpled with accordion folds, a victimized article of clothing of unwanted undesired staining due to my overactive sweat glands. Avant-garde men's dress code: a crinkled and sweat-drenched shirt?

And here was good old peripheral vision doing its job, intercepting, even though I tried so hard to fixedly stare ahead, to evade the monolith, a skyscraper casting its long shadow, internalized since childhood, an adolescent sentimental association, a timeless shadow on that dirty kitchen wall. My miniature hand reaching for the handle. From its towering perspective I must have seemed like one more kneeling worshipper, no identity, blending in, blindly bowing down before this seraphic being. Yes, it threw a heavy shadow and left a permanent mark. Etching itself on my subconscious mind. A place of permanence. An uninvited guest that just would not leave. Even now I could envision the vast richness of its interior, beyond the impenetrable vault door only granting access to those bestowed with the safe combination. Camouflaged behind the state-of-the-art security, combination-based lock, and vault door with sliding bolts, an opportunity for self-abandonment. No restrictions. Unbridled freedom. Rise to impulsivity. Riotous behavior.

Unethical thoughts entered my mind, chipping away at my brittle foundation. The apparatus began to glow with luminous intensity; all the while my inquisitive mind could not resist fantasizing, craving a sugar-sweetened beverage, or a powder puff pastry sprinkled generously with sugar, to open the door and spot the familiar trustworthy Big Chill emblem with the name written in hieroglyphic font.

I craved a treat for my valiant efforts. I wanted it so much I knew I could not have it. Knowing perfectly well it would never be just one. I would never be able to consume just one. One would never be enough to solidify my nerves on my Don Quixote journey to the party room of my condominium building. I sighed. My feet picked up pace again. I was rebelling against my cravings. Denial. Denial which triggered a remembrance. An episodic recollection, pouncing on me. A postcard from the past. Two dots blinking on an interconnected graph of pain. She was on my mind again. What started as a mere thought shortly molded into a character sketch, a contour drawing with overlaying multitudinous lines, until a facial composite emerged. Her face, the face that gave me lifelong restlessness.

Who was she you might ask? Once upon a time, when I weighed a hundred and thirty pounds, I had a slightly overweight girlfriend. A good-natured person who fell for me, and who knows, maybe I would have fallen for her if it was not for that one minor problem. To me at the time, it was her only inferior quality, making her incomplete in my eyes. One step away from perfection, and madly in love with me. What was I to do as a selfish, pitiful creature that I was? I broke her heart, unable to give her what she sought after—the return of affection.

No kind words were a substitute for her pain; niceties do not equal compensation when you break someone's heart. Before we parted ways, I remember she asked me if I found her attractive. I replied that I did not because she was much bigger than I would have preferred. It is funny how weight, like extra emotional baggage, can keep you from loving someone. But it does; there is no denying it.

Trust me, dear reader, I know what you are thinking. And you are right. I learned about unconditional love, compromise, and reality of living a tad bit too late, way after being diagnosed with irregular levels of cholesterol and suffering through and surviving my first heart attack. She was already long gone.

At that time, I was a student of media-promoted negative body image, allowing society to spoon feed me, consumerism consuming me. I denied someone a part of me because I was merely a product of superficiality, chasing after the wrong things, letting her slip away. And after my fall from fame, I will never forget the sobering words someone said to me when I gained the first hundred pounds, "Welcome to the real-world asshole... no one thinks you are the life of the party. You are not the greatest gift bestowed upon humanity; just another fat bastard..."

Now isolated within these concrete confines, I cannot help but reminisce and contemplate what could have been. In a cruel twist of fate, I was what I once rejected. Continuously sliding down an endless slope. Stranded in downward motion, possessor of a single move, resigned to my spiral of poisonous thoughts, a torturous reprise. Complete loss of control over my life, failure to remember the last time I had a good day. And it all started before the audience stopped laughing. It started when I lost her.

I reached the phone, dialing two numbers, one to confirm my comeback performance tonight, and the other, her number which had not changed in years. She accepted the invitation with a slightly quivering voice. My own throat constricted when I heard her voice, turning on the valves, tear ducts nearly flooding my condominium. I was extra nervous now, seeing her tonight after all this time and the audience's reaction to my weight gain. I would have to prepare accordingly. Naturally, there were expectations for me to do some of my old material. It made sense; they booked me on what little weight my name still carried in this industry. They were paying a tribute, homage to the past; I was a throwback, a dinosaur, hardly a modernist trying to modernize the world. But I did have a surprise in-store for them. A single self-referential joke, making fun of my own asinine hilariousness, therefore anticipating my attacker's advancing movements and checkmating him into a corner. I wanted to dismantle the governing body, The Audience, with a singular punchline securing my place, proving them wrong, a legacy left untarnished.

Do you think me excessive? You think things have changed. Sure, the world constantly changes, certain conversational topics become old and obsolete with time; fatness is not one of them. Still a rapidly circulating conversational piece. The society we are all part of is really a merciless jury that is trying awfully hard to ridicule and disprove of you. Sure, it is simple-mindedness and a part of what I like to call 21st-century ever-so-growing ignorance, but that is just how it is. I cannot blame them, I used to be one of them, it would take a lengthier period for things to truly change, and in the meantime, I have to prepare to deflect their criticism, to come up with the perfect joke, the most perfect punchline directly tackling all my critics all at once. The perfect retort. My magnus opus. Right in the center of all my work. An astounding similarity to my inebriated father's favourite inebriated writer's plans for his magnus opus, "The Voyage That Never Ends," a summation of all his life's work, with his masterpiece novel, *Under the Volcano*, as the centerpiece.

Confronting your critics is hardly a conventional method of gaining acceptance. But if done with finesse, a delicate balance of comedy and slice-of-life commentary, laughter if gained, would bring it all together, a key ingredient to softening the blow. Instead of being a clichéd angry comic firing back, you would rise to celebrity status for your ingenuity, celebrated for your extraordinary wit, having chosen the experimental, bypassing the more familiar.

This is what I was banking on. One joke to change the course of my personal history of recent failures. A man possessed. In my last-ditch effort, inevitably heading toward self-destruction, or stardom. The rope suddenly stopped moving. I found myself standing before my front door. A milestone, but also the end of my assisted acceleration. From here on I would have to fend for myself, using walls or anything else I could hold onto.

Out in the hallway, my thoughts went back to The Audience. It was a suicide mission to take them on. In my state of decrepitude, overweight and aging ungracefully, to take on a room full of people, no singular opponents, no one-on-one battles, a whole slew of them. I knew what awaited me once I stepped onto that stage, it was always the same, at the beginning of every act, always a friendly expression on their faces and a slight touch of a devilish glimmer in their eyes, indicating to me as a comedian that if I slipped, found myself wounded and bleeding profusely, they would shred me to pieces without so much as a hint of mercy. The Audience anxiously awaits such a moment to strike you down. Each laugh is a confirmation of the fact that you fit in; each silent reaction, a sigh, or a boo, shoves you further in life's trash receptacle as a defective human being, an unworthy performer.

My raspy wheezing filled the hallway. I could tell my body was on the fritz, starting to malfunction. I had shortness of breath, a pair of struggling lungs and a birthing sensation of a fatal cough trying to claw its way out of my throat. Can you blame me for passing up the double-helix stairwell? The only condominium building around these parts with one, drawing inspiration from French Renaissance and Da Vinci's own creation for Château de Chambord. Nice to look at, but a royal pain in the arse to one's ascent or descent.

The elevator arrived timely, greeting me with a dinging noise and another plaque, this time an Elevator Capacity Plate, also in a hieroglyphic font identical to my Big Chill refrigerator.

The doors closed; the apparatus began descending, the steel cable did not snap, there was no plummeting below for the single overweight occupant. I watched transfixed as floor numbers lit up, and grew dark, and lit up again, a zigzagging pattern, thinking about how I would amend the personal history of my historic failures, rewrite whole sections, modified to my liking, about the audience's receptivity below.

I always had this theory. That people who come to watch a comedy show, or any show for that matter, are simply individuals intensely combating the awkward silences in their lives. Silence that sneaked into their lives over time. A handful of years. Once the honeymoon period ended, their compatibility was suddenly tested, purposive hurt introduced to the loving relationship, from civilized to aggressive, caffeinated caged and shouting, shrieking and violent, craving reconciliation sex, riding that carousel more times they cared to discuss, until one day they just lost their zest for the whole thing, giving in, giving up, settling for marital unhappiness, responsibilities of raising children and mundaneness of everyday life. These people felt alone even when they were together. They wanted noise-cancelling headphones for their home life, white noise for the stinging and invading pain. They were way past talking to each other, trying, putting in the time and effort, past exchanging ideas, discussing vast topics ranging from corrupt politicians, inflating prices, city workers going on strike, whose marriage was falling apart due to yet another infidelity. No, these individuals have had their fill. They depleted the resources of communication amongst themselves. It no longer offered excitation. They wanted a tryst, a midnight rendezvous, to be tongue-tied for an evening, not having to worry about puritanical appearances, acceptable behavior, placing place settings and feeding their children with cherubic faces. Trading paradisiacal palisades of their guarded community, the spiritless suburbia for subterranean devilry. These were philistines, not patrons of the arts. They merely wanted escapism. A stranger to fill their heads. A morally corrupt stand-up comic delivering the goods: immorality, immodesty, and obscenity. Food for thought, nutritive to their stale lives. Perhaps something they could even discuss behind locked doors, back in the privacy of their safe, secure homes.

Anyway, it is just a theory.

You know, doing stand up all these years, something I never got used to were the establishments themselves. A common reoccurring problem with most comedy clubs is the outdated décor, derivative patterns, overlapping and mismatched colors, an interior designer's disastrous vision, inverted measurements, and absence of spatial balance. Let us not forget excessive lighting, powerful projectors providing more than efficient illumination, enough light for you to be able to see gathering moisture on the performer's face and the fine layers of dust floating through the air which makes you self-consciously review if there is enough clean air in this facility in the first place to even breathe. Those dust collecting red theater curtains certainly did not help, placed there purely for the sake of adding that bit of theatrical flair. Particulate matter and incinerating lights, yes, those I could do without. The rest, I missed terribly. The venues being crowded and compressed with people, a myriad of servers zigzagging about with drink trays, camera crews capturing crystal clear moving images, a self-contained world unlike any other that does not stop spinning until the comedian on stage starts performing.

Tonight's venue could not be more different. On the plus side, the décor was not as atrocious, and there was sterility to the air. Unfortunately, it was also missing all the things I fondly described above. This was after all the party room of a condominium building, not an actual comedy club, a scaled-down version meant to accommodate a smaller audience with makeshift curtains and no camera crews. This comeback would be spread by word of mouth, hopefully still leading to greater business opportunities.

After spending some time waiting for my cue—allowing me time to jot down my joke—

they finally called for me. The foray toward the microphone was comprised of slow, deliberate steps. In my peripheral vision, I could see their eagerness growing. An inhospitable taste permeated my mouth, my muscles twitched; I had my repellent against their cynicism ready in the pocket of my dirty sweatpants, sanctuary to sweat-stained scribbles with the faultless joke. I imagined myself stripped bare before this lawless authority, suppressing a secret weapon, safeguarding these scraps, biding my time until I can reveal them, unveiling them at the moment of least expectation, catching The Audience completely off guard. Just before they display their jagged teeth, showing me the emotional poverty of humanity. The Emptiness. The Imbecility. Before they can entertain themselves with their own howling, crude amusement gained from taunting the performer. The people's government, the giant pressing machine flattening dissidents, operated by primitive peasants, shadowing my every action in anticipation of delivering repeated blows on behalf of the simple-minded society they represent; hoping and praying that the final heavy attack to my undersides will do the job of hemorrhaging my heart.

The air suddenly did not feel so sterile, more so tampered with, stifling and suffocating. I would have gritted my teeth if my jaw were not so tightly clenched. The audience's incessant chatter amongst themselves deafened me. A myriad of murmuring heads. And those unbearable lights, obliterating visibility, blinding my organ of sight. Mucus steadily ran toward the corners of my tightly interwoven lips. I skimmed the room for the last time with my hypersensitive eyes. So much pain had assembled within me. I was bursting. So much that on some level it was liberating to just give in. To cease fighting and embrace this pain. Handing myself over. Relinquishing. This room was my reliquary preserving my remains.

I felt a spreading pain, a series of spasms that brought me to a standstill, I was doing my best to be the receiver of this unconventional gift, but was it a gift or a curse? I felt a pressure. I felt deformed, defeated, and drained. It was near impossible to generate new, or conserve old energy. A severe subtraction of fully functional organs. I feebly attempted to articulate my distress, gesticulating with my hands, but to no avail. The human factor in those seats showed no remorse, occupying their thrones with obscene comments right on the tips of their protruding tongues, recalled and retrieved just in time to accompany my staggering and struggling. Things had come full circle for me. I was staring directly at a freshly dug grave. Earth excavated in my honor. My final resting place. The microphone serving as a burial marker. The best funeral photographer in the business snapping away during the open-casket funeral service, capturing expertly the funereal pallor on my embalmed face. Colonnade of pallbearer's hands extended above their heads, moving centipede-like, transporting my casket.

I stared at them defiantly. These representatives of a world that has failed to comprehend my genius pulverizing me with their eyes. I poised myself, aware that these might be my last spoken words, a culmination of a comedian's career, a few relevant words of lasting importance. My joke. The set-up and punchline.

[Dear Readers: Please Insert Joke Here]

After the punchline, I remained still for what seemed to me an eternity. Then a misstep followed, a slip, spattering the stage with my convulsing body. Sprawled. Guilty of public littering. I suddenly had an inordinate desire to see the summits of holy mountains, hopeful the soaring heights would ward off the evil below. Sadly, I was not in optimal climbing condition, having reached the lowest of the lows, the stage floor. I could not possibly get any lower and death was steadfastly approaching. My time was up. The pied piper was calling my name. This was the price I had to pay. Myocardial infarction claiming me after years of service as a dedicated overeater.

I once went to a photographer. He looked me in the eyes and said, "You could look at the devil with these and not even blink." I was looking at them now, The Audience, the clamorous mob, unblinking. The room erupted, a Roman amphitheatre vibrating with customary clapping and cheering mixed with bloodcurdling screams for paramedics. The Audience was devoid of a matching reaction. While I was desperate for uniformity, seeking assurances, substantive evidence, a revolutionary reaction of identicalness, a phenomenon like no other. The lack of balance tremendously tormented me. I began to drift off, still lacking the fundamental knowledge so important in deducing the source of their laughter, my joke, or my second this-time-possibly-fatal heart attack.

# MURDER ON CHRISTMAS EVE

MICHAEL WALKED OVER to the enormous bay window. He had a hankering to watch the sunset from inside this stereotypical mafioso mansion, which took its architectural cues from kingpins like Al Capone and his hideaways from federal agents and rival mafia families. The sun was slowly setting in the wintry distance. Spilling redness. Bloodying the surrounding snow-covered land canvas. Spreading that breath-taking crimson as more snow started to fall. One of those picturesque sights perfectly worthy of pictorial format.

He stiffened from a draft. A penetrating gust from an improperly installed window. Michael examined the time on his wristwatch, then left the poorly insulated window with its miniature mistral wind and walked over to the antique mahogany Victorian-era coffee table where he generously helped himself to a vodka eggnog infusion, sending his cup to the bottom of the bowl, a deep diving dunk until the sweetish alcoholic mixture reached the brim and overflowed, dampening his sleeve slightly in the process with the viscous alcoholic nectar inside.

A hearty sip followed from a swan-shaped mug while he fished in his pockets for a handkerchief. Once located, Michael wiped the dampened spot on his sleeve before he returned the now syrupy-sticky handkerchief back to that same pocket. With mug in hand, he walked back over to the picturesque sight at the bay window. The sun had now set. A storm raged somewhere close by. Within a minute the weather turned, significantly altering the landscape, intensifying everything outside, bringing along severe snow and treacherous conditions. Even the Japanese topiary gardens he admired earlier had now disappeared, everything fully entombed in white.

Michael gulped another mouthful of the cup's contents and walked deeper into the room, away from the window and its spectacular snow scene, his swan-shaped mug purposefully left behind, placed on the closed lid of a grand piano situated near the window, guaranteeing a water ring. He knew the water would seep in, staining the lid, the finish unsalvageable if not gotten to in time by the owner of this prestigious mansion; the owner unfortunately indisposed at this very crucial, potentially waterlogged-piano-lid type of moment. Oh yes, indisposed indeed, resting peacefully: a motionless corpse sprawled out near his killer's scuffed leather shoes.

A candy cane protruded from the corpse's left eyeball while a steady blood rivulet seeped out and stained the antique Persian carpet beneath the slowly cooling body. Michael nonchalantly looked down at the corpse. A killer admiring his handiwork.

*Snow and more fucking snow. Christmas… a holiday everyone is supposed to like. And those who hate it quickly become outcasts. But I for one not only hate it, but everything that it represents. Just look at that fucking snow. I wish I were on the Cayman Islands right now instead of being stuck in a blizzard in this empty house. And thanks to this asshole, now just another exterminated loudmouth, I am stuck here for a good long while. Forgive me, dear reader, I am a bit cranky. Still adjusting to these newly prescribed anti-depressants, which supposedly help with stabilization of the mind. Side effects include: severe fucking with one's concentration. You should have seen what I did to the doctor who prescribed me these. Unfortunately, the writer of this story, as well as my life story, is lacking the masculinity to depict it as it actually happened. But just between the two of us while he's stepped out of the room, what he failed to jot down was the scene in the doctor's office, a great and gruesome bloody mess of a scene. It is almost ironic the publishing company would allow a description of a corpse with a candy cane sticking through the eye socket in all its graphic glory, but not this. Hypocrites. You see something wrong with this? Because I do. Anyway, back to this doctor prick and what I didn't do to him, but actually did. I broke every single one of his fingers. One for every time he used the word "depression," or any of its synonyms. And believe me when I say he used more than ten. It got to the point where I had to break his toes. But I let him off the hook after a while. The smell was sickening. The bastard pissed all over himself, his chair, and the floor. Now you might ask why I caved in and took the pills in the end. Well at first, I didn't see it the way he saw it, didn't agree with what he had to say. Now I have come around. I should probably send him a "I Hope You Feel Better Soon"*

*Hallmark card. They really did help with the mood swings, which I was getting more often than some dames I know. Sure, my concentration might be a bit off, but this might even out in time. For now, I'm giving the pills a try, following the doctor's advice. Since the writer is still not back, this would be the part where he'd tell you about how I gripped the corpse by the ankles, walked backwards and dragged it out of the room. The floor becoming instantly bloodied with, well… blood. The kitchen would replace the living room, a change of scenery for the cadaver. I would try to catch my breath, wiping my perspiration-covered forehead with the vodka eggnog-stained handkerchief. Don't ask me how come there is so much blood. Beats me where it's all coming from. I only poked him in the eye. I just know his maid isn't going to like this mess. Moving along… after this brief breather of catching my breath I would resume my hold on the body, open the door leading to the cellar and proceed to drag the corpse down into that cobwebbed catacomb. A dog, the owner's dog, would follow me closely behind.*

*Not that I noticed it until I reached the bottom, carelessly dropping the body. I would say something sadistically sarcastic like, "Weren't much help to your owner were you pal?" The dog would whimper a little. I would bend down, retrieve the bloodied candy cane from the corpse's eye and throw it to the dog. Another sadistically sarcastic remark from my lips along the lines of, "Here you go, mutt. Gourmet dog food courtesy of your more than generous owner." The dog would instantly devour it. And if you dear gullible fools think for one split second that he didn't know there was blood on that sugary peppermint treat representing Jesus' purity, you are in denial, folks. Will you look at me? Just look at me, ranting away. Rant to paper method of storytelling. Not good. Not good at all. But this is what happens, folks, when you have an absentee writer, barricading himself in his bathroom, over-analyzing the same descriptive sentence about a fucking sunset. So I am taking over. Getting one over on the writer while he tries so hard to find the perfect words, construct the perfect sentence, wanting to impress the literary hordes and give his entrusted Editor a headache by repeating himself repeatedly, vomitus of verbal tautology. He has no idea I am doing this internal monologue, running amok, taking the reins of this project. You must also be wondering when this slow perfectionist is going to get to giving up a few details about the dead guy now relocated to the cellar. You need this information to find out exactly what you should feel toward him, the dead guy. Should you feel sorry since he is the victim and hate me for slay-ing a good man? Or congratulate me for ridding the world of a good-for-nothing son of a bitch? I hate to be the bearer of bad news, but there are no good guys in this story. Just criminals—various degrees of deceitful, cunning, and despicable individuals. But for your sake, I will help you out. Simplify the matter. Help you root for someone. With this said, you might as well root for me. (Pause) I am sorry for the narrative pause; I just had an outburst of seemingly pointless anger, kicking the corpse vio-lently, enjoying the sound of his ribs breaking under the force of my foot, then stopping as suddenly as I had started. It may seem pointless, but that couldn't be further from the truth. As soon as I begin to tell you my story, you'll see that my present actions are more than justified. First, let me tell you a bit about myself, and how I got tangled up with this asshole. Who am I? Just a simple narrow-minded criminal, or is there dimension and depth to me? Maybe I am just a cardboard cut-out. Let's give a breather to this narrative technique and find out. I'd rather show for once than tell. Keep in mind, I am no pretentious word scribbler who takes an infinity to jot down one fucking sentence, I get to the point I am trying to make. And if you find it violent, hurtful, and too realistic you can stop reading it, I won't be offended. This is real life.*

A small apartment with hairline cracks along the walls and an unmistakable feeling of desolation. A pair of suitcases rest near the door. My former wife, I mean, *Michael's* current wife occupies the only chair sitting behind the only table. She is a knowledgeable woman, a woman of the world—intelligent, cultured, a person happy to oblige you if she cares enough about you. Her only problem is she is the type of woman you love for her mind and not for her sexual appeal, though she is charming. *Was this right? Did I do this correctly? I might need some practice.*

Michael walks through the door, instantly notices her.

"Where were you?" she says. "Answer me, dammit!"

He gestures with his hand for her to remain calm. "Don't raise your voice. There's no need to raise your voice."

She looks at him with plain disbelief. "No reason... no *reason*? You are out until the early hours of the night, and I shouldn't worry?"

"If I knew you were so worried, I would have called."

"God, you are pitiful. All you ever do is twist my words around until they lose all their meaning. Just a smart ass with his arsenal of smart-ass remarks. I am so sick of them. Of you. You used to be a writer. A writer, Michael. Now what are you?"

"I am still a writer." He smiles broadly.

"To call yourself a writer you actually need to write. You don't do that anymore. You hang around low-life sleazes, like that degenerate gambler Timothy Price, and you are becoming stupider. Just look at the words you use. Nothing but profanities."

"He is a friend."

"I am your friend! Your best friend. Your wife. And I am sick and tired of your goddamn stupidity. See what you made me do? Your foulness is rubbing off on me."

"Hey... come on... come here."

"Don't you dare. Tell me right now. Tell me what I want to know. Are you willing to change?"

"I don't know how you think I used to be; I am what I am now."

"Is that your runaround way of saying no?"

"You got it, toots. Now are you going to make dinner, or should I grab something from the corner deli?"

"No, Michael, I am not."

*And there you have it. The beginning. Well… close enough. That was the last time I saw my wife. Her skittishness and nervousness, the way she took the room in for the last time, wringing her hands, strangling all life from them, running those same hands through her graying thinning hair… I hate that memory. I hate that it stuck around. Constantly reminding me of itself. Its existence lodged in my head. Replaying everything in slow motion. The way she stood up, walked over to the front door, took a suitcase in each hand, and left the premises. I remember I ran to the door, a last-ditch effort to hear her high heels out in the hallway. I forgot about the carpet. The carpet muffled all sound. So, I stood there like an idiot. Listening. All the while, she was long gone. Either this tale will help to humanize me a little or make me even more of an asshole than I*

*already seem like. Killing a man and all. And will*
*you just look at that dog, licking its chops from that*
*candy cane. Hey, if you were here you might look*
*on with perverse interest as well. Not something*
*you see every day. I know I promised you to get to*
*the matter at hand. The corpse on the floor. I just*
*wanted to tell you something about the past, about*
*me. When she left, it was what these shrinks call the*
*"trigger effect" and no matter how bad I was before,*
*I was worse after, and everything that happened*
*from that day on, happened because of that day. I*
*stopped living for a while. Then I started up again,*
*but I wasn't the same, making bad decisions and*
*amassing dangerous acquaintances. Spending all*
*my time downtown with the drunks, prostitutes,*
*and trash. The neon lights became my guideways.*
*I mapped out the course from one bar to the next.*
*One night in a drunken frenzy at a seedy watering*
*hole where I was finishing the last glass of whisky*
*I could legitimately pay for, a guy stumbled in,*
*crazed, out of his mind, pulled out a gun and shot*
*the place up. Talk about chaos and commotion.*

*Screams, bodies and blood everywhere, and just me and the sharply dressed gentleman next to me continuing to drink at the bar like nothing happened. He complimented me on my calmness and bought me another. I didn't know him. But I knew what he was. Once I accepted that drink it was too late. Sure, I saw the warning signs, but my life was over. I'd lost her, I was an aimless drifter, self destructive, looking for trouble. That man took me under his wing. Showed me the ropes. Introduced me to the trade. In no time I was doing odd jobs for the mob. Odd jobs soon turned into specific jobs. The sharply dressed gentleman then introduced me to The Boss. He was his right-hand man, and I was his. He trusted me. And that trust got me my first serious assignment. Surveillance. To tail The Boss's main squeeze, Alessandra, and, if caught in the act, to get rid of her and whoever she was seeing. I was the guy who handled things that needed handling. Old fashioned American boy with a passion for blackjack, disdain for the law and love of fast women. And this wasn't just any old job, this was*

*an opportunity for advancement—forget ripping
off easy marks, blasting and shoving off, this was
a high-class broad that came with a hefty price tag,
this would open doors. It always sounds easier
than it actually is. That's how they get to sell it to
you. I tailed her for a while, never much to report,
she was either innocent or too smart for me. I was
about to throw in the towel, pack up and go see The
Boss with my final report when she did something
different (if you call going inside a hotel different).
I followed her, tipped the miserable prick manning
the ship and got her room number. I couldn't believe
it. I had the jitters. I'd never murdered anyone
before. Undoubtedly, this was all about to change,
I had my instructions, and I didn't dare show up
empty-handed to the adultery party. I was packing
an unlicensed Beretta with a screwed-on silencer
and grip tape on the handle, a pair of black tactical
gloves on my hands. I reached the room and lock
picked my way inside. There she was. Stark naked.
Mounting some chump. They had no idea I was
there. Watching them. Moving. Moaning. When*

*they switched positions, that's when I pulled the trigger. Bang. A blood geyser. Cranial splattering. He coated the walls. The sheets. Her. She was so stunned she didn't even scream. She just pushed the dead man away, snatched a crumpled pack of cigarettes and a lighter from the nightstand and walked over to the chair near the bed, never caring that my gun followed her every movement. Alessandra then sat down, crossed her legs, and lit up a cigarette, looking me up and down. I should have shot her right then and there. Instead, I decided to open my mouth and ask her a question. A mistake that resulted in this mess here.*

"Who's the guy?"

"A paying customer."

"Greedy."

"So, he finally decided to put a tail on me."

"He did."

"Took him a while. Almost had me convinced he trusted me."

"Evidently, not enough. Otherwise, I would

have never got the gig."

"Don't be naïve, you aren't the only one, they never send just one guy. No matter how good you are. Even the tail has a tail."

"So, if I don't kill you, they will kill me."

"That's the idea."

*I speechlessly stared at her body like a prepubescent schoolboy. I couldn't help myself. I mean, what would you have done in my position? Face to face with a striking beauty, stripped and puffing seductively on her cigarette. I second guessed myself. And while I churned things over, she took a final, long drag on her cigarette, expelled the perfect smoke ring, uncrossed those runway model legs and lowered her blood-spattered hand.*

"Don't…"

"I wonder what kind of lover you are. Hopefully not the selfish type. I've always believed pleasure should belong to all participants."

*I don't know why I let her start, why I led her on instead of easing her pain and simply getting it over with. Maybe it was the power, a perverse pleasure in having so much control. I had her life in my hands, after all. Her hopes, her dreams, her fate... Look now, I knew she was an actress performing a role. Acting out her part. But as she dreamily brought herself to an orgasm, massaging herself in all the right areas, I still found it impossible to look away. I stood, stared, and noticed. I noticed her nails, filed to perfection. Her cunning, sensual mouth. I noticed her insane hunger for life. She was willing to do anything to stay alive. And there I was, a voyeur. A peeping tom peeking in on a private moment of sexual self pleasure. She moaned louder. I noticed her breathing increase, her hand movements become more vigorous; having reached the point of no return, she moved her hips forward, and arched her strong sweat covered body in that worn down chair, making me bear witness to an explosive climax the likes of which I'd never seen before. Explosive. That's the word. But I was soon over it. She came, and I came to my senses. Awoke from my spellbound trance. No more standing in one spot staring. I'd been generous enough, having allowed her that bit of pleasure before a great amount of pain. Her time was up.*

*If only I'd stuck with that sentiment and pulled the trigger…*

"Did you enjoy the show? You seem like the sort to enjoy such a thing. Observer of human nature."

"I did while it lasted. Unfortunately…"

"… our time is up."

"That's just it."

"Before you get all trigger happy. I know where he keeps the money."

*She must have taken me for a fool. A real capital S schmuck. But it didn't matter because she was right all along—I'd been tailed. A couple of goons sent to make sure I didn't botch this up. They had a time limit, dictated by The Boss; so while I thought her time was up, it should have been up a long time ago. Now both of ours was up, and I knew this by the turning of the handle behind me. And since the writer is trying to impress his Editor with little cute references of what sunsets look like in Moncton, New Brunswick—because get this, this is where the Editor is from—still trying to perfect the opening 'enormous bay window' scene, I will have to pull double duty as narrator and exposition writer (although I already did that with a flashback scene to my failed marriage didn't I? And unlike that lazy prick I always keep exposition writing in the present tense. Screw that third person impersonal bullshit) because what followed was a close quarters shootout.*

"What is it?"

"Everything and nothing at the same time."

Michael gestures for her to stay silent. Her whole being projects uneasiness. She gets up from the chair. Michael gestures again, this time for her to stand back. She huddles helplessly against the back wall. There is a clicking sound. The knob fully turns. The door bursts open. Michael aims the gun at the intruder's face, and fires twice. The intruder fires a single shot before he collapses on the floor. The bullet collides with the pillow on the bed. Alessandra frantically screams.

"It's good you decided to get out of that chair. Now get dressed."

Michael swiftly picks up the hastily removed dress lying abandoned on the floor. Without losing momentum, he throws it to the slightly stunned Alessandra. All it takes is that gesture and the look on his face for her to realize the seriousness of the situation. While she dresses, he crouches next to the corpse and turns the bloody head sideways—an ear device treacherously reveals itself. She looks at him quizzically while continuing to clothe herself.

"Familiar to you? Or are you just checking for wax?"

"He has an earpiece."

"Meaning?"

"Meaning there's a lot more of them, and we will be lucky to get out of here with our lives intact."

"Well, aren't you an optimist."

He ignores her words, walks over to the window and notices two conspicuous cars below.

"We have to move. They will move quicker once they don't hear from him."

"Can't you reply for him?" She ties the straps around her neck, securing the dress in place.

"I am not an impersonator."

She hurriedly grabs her purse from the nightstand.

"Let's hope you are the better hitman."

Michael opens the door in one fluid motion. Alessandra hides behind him. He grasps her hand firmly as he steps out into the hallway. They move unitedly, a grafted togetherness, moving toward the elevator, with both noticing upon shortening the distance, an arm's length away from the button, the elevator already steadily rising, and now looming dangerously close to their floor.

"Catering?"

He looks in the direction of the hallway.

"Take the left stairwell, and I will take the right."

His suggestion arouses a look of horror.

"You're leaving me?!"

"We stand a better chance if we separate."

"What am I supposed to do when I meet one of them?!"

He looks at her, callously. "You are a seductress. Seduce. And then shoot him in the crotch with this."

He reaches inside his jacket and retrieves a small calibre weapon. Her hands tremble as she takes the weapon from him. He turns away, and heads for the stairwell to the right. She remains immovable in her hopelessness and continues to watch him. He briefly pauses near the door, makes eye contact with her, then disappears behind it.

Once Michael enters the right stairwell and the door shuts behind him, he instantly realizes he is not alone. He hears noises. As above, so below him. He feels claustrophobically cornered. A face manifests itself from concealment of the upper stairwell directly above him, a face that's part of a whole, a body in malicious motion, with injurious intentions, a malevolent arm swings forward, hand grasps, finger squeezes... the trigger, part of a gun grasped tightly in that hand, as it releases fury, wildly uncoordinated shots springing forth and striking the walls all around Michael, but astonishingly never him directly. He never moves, standing still, remaining deadly calm, until in a perfectly reactionary manner he discharges his silenced weapon, eliminating the above threat before he backs away and turns his weapon on the threat below.

*I apologize, dear readers, if this next part isn't up to par, but it did require a fair share of guess-work on my part. What may read as a false narrative is merely me grasping at straws, trying to fill in the unfilled, tell what was untold to me.*

Alessandra cautiously opens the door to the left stairwell, but immediately she is grabbed and slammed hard against the wall. A barrel of a handgun gets pressed underneath her chin. She attempts to swallow but the henchman's meaty hand repositions the gun, blocking her attempt. She quickly becomes breathless, gasping for air. Michael's advice comes back to her. She gently forces the barrel of the gun down with her hand, swallows the lump in her throat and alters her usual tonal frequency, tuning it to the more alluring; the more seductive.

"If you are going to kill me, wouldn't you rather have a bit of fun with me first? Unless you prefer my corpse with those necrophiliac fetishes some men have."

He slaps her across her face. A little stream of blood runs down from the corner of her mouth.

"Forgive me. Why did I think necrophilia? You are clearly into more aristocratic fetishes, like battering women. One of those men who like to hit. Well, go ahead. Hit me some more."

He repeatedly hits her several times. She pretends to enjoy his abuse.

"I said hit me, don't slap me."

He punches her at her command. A dark

discoloration forms instantly on her cheek.

"You like that don't you, you pervert. Don't you want to kiss my sensual bloody lips?"

Alessandra stretches her pinkish-hued tongue out and enticingly licks the blood from her upper lip. He kisses her hard. They exchange saliva and blood as he gropes her chest. Her hand reaches into her purse discreetly, retrieves the small caliber weapon and fires without any second thought. She leaves the moaning, woman-battering mafioso henchman behind to bleed to death as she takes the stairs, changing stairwells along the way and finally running into Michael as he presses another henchman's face brutally into the wall and fires a single point-blank shot. Blood sprays and runs down the wall. He finally turns to her.

"You survived. Congratulations."

"You left me you bastard!"

He returns his weapon to its holster-prison under his arm.

"Watch your tone with me. I am the only person who can get you out of here alive."

He opens the door, discreetly looks about

both hallways, and leads the way to the Garbage Chute Room, pulling back the door.

"Ladies first."

"Burn in hell."

*Instead of showing you the scene, would it be wrong if I made a comparison? The garbage chute symbolized a descent into something that could only equal the lowest depths. Yes, I'd say that's exactly what it symbolized. A spot-on comparison. For the more morbidly curious, sticklers for details and so on, questioning achievability and such, imagine a festering smell of rotting flesh, imagine an escalator to Dante's Inferno, imagine a noxious hot hell. Perfectly possible, but something that should be avoidable at all costs. Of course, we ended up in the basement of the building, not hell, where we stole some poor bastard's brand-new car, driving the story forward and bringing it closer to the present.*

Michael grips the wheel firmly, deliberately presses down on the gas pedal, pushes the stolen vehicle to its limits. Alessandra occupies the passenger seat. She keeps touching her bloody lips. He finally notices her repetitive gestures; notices she is hurt. He takes out a handkerchief and throws it to her. *I always had a thing for throwing things to people, or at them.*

"Wipe the blood from your face. It draws too much unneeded attention."

She looks down at the handkerchief, contemplates if she should accept his brutish gesture, a momentary pause before she succumbs, wraps the handkerchief around her hand and dabs at her bloodied lip. The white handkerchief slowly soaks up the blood and turns pink. Alessandra takes it away from her face and wrings it in her hands.

"You are just afraid people might think it's your handiwork."

Michael slows the car down, timing the brake release with a brutal slap across Alessandra's face. Her lower lip splits open even more, gushing blood which fills her mouth and stains her teeth.

"What's next, you are going to bruise my bruises?"

"Open your mouth."

He forces it open for her. One hand pries her

mouth open while the other shoves the barrel of his gun inside. Her body violently jerks as the weapon slithers down her throat.

"You see, we have a little problem. I think you are withholding something. Actually, 'I think' isn't the right phrase. I know you are withholding something from me."

Alessandra attempts to speak. The gun prevents her from doing just that. She really tries to speak, but she just spews bloody saliva and incomprehensibilities. Tears start to run down her face. Michael watches her, unmoved by the sight. She sheds more tears. Tears that follow in the tracks of their predecessors. He finally removes the gun from her mouth. The barrel is coated with sticky saliva and traces of red lipstick. She breaks out into a raging cough. He pays her no mind and wipes the gun clean on his pant leg. She finally regains control of herself and turns to him. Their eyes meet.

"Do you hate me now?"

"Hate? No, I despise you."

Alessandra gives Michael a look, a mix of arousal and hatred. He reciprocates. Lust overtakes them. He forces her toward him. His lips entwine with hers. She half-heartedly fights him off, then swiftly surrenders to her overwhelming urge. A few minutes of pure animal passion, and it is all over. All that built up frustration satisfied; their desire disperses like the carbon monoxide from the stolen vehicle's tailpipe. They sit back down in their seats. Both breathe hard and try their best to arrange their clothes, make themselves presentable again. He takes a pack of cigarettes from his jacket pocket, retrieves a single smoke and lights it. She turns the front-view mirror toward herself, takes out a red lipstick from her purse and carefully traces her lips with it.

"How much does he have in the safe?"

"Enough."

"Never is there such a thing as enough when you are dealing with people like us. Our hearts pump greed faster than blood."

He stares ahead, through the windshield

and past it, absorbed, lost in thought, trying to detect mobility in the wintry wasteland ahead. She watches him with unconcealed hunger, waiting for his mystification to wear off, feeling the pangs, experiencing full on parasitic uncontrollable itching for capital. He empties his mouth from the latest drag's chemical contents before turning to her, his mind set on something concrete.

"Either we run, or we try to get this money."

*This is how you create tension and write a realistic scene. But here comes the hack, defeated and tired of redrafting his 'enormous bay window' scene. He is cheating. Jumping ahead in the narrative. Working on the scene I just shared with you. Let's hear his god awful politically-correct version of the same events.*

Michael drives. Alessandra occupies the passenger seat, next to him but oblivious to his state of mind, worrying herself with her own worrisome thoughts, all the while touching her bloodied lip repeatedly and obsessively. Both are silent. The tension inside the car constricts them, driver and passenger, nervousness replacing talkativeness. Suddenly, her words pierce through the established vocal immobility, secured by mutual agreement, mutual silence, cutting through the human noiselessness inside the vehicle.

"You are just going to drive all night without uttering a word?"

"Talking ruins things. You talked and now look where it's gotten us."

"You are the one who decided to listen."

"I did. Like an idiot, meddling in a private affair that did not concern me."

"Well, now that you have me all to yourself, I am honestly surprised you wouldn't want to pull over at once and force yourself on me for all the trouble I've caused you."

"You'd like that, wouldn't you? You live for this drama. Probably find it exciting?"

"I enjoy turning heads. Commanding a room full of dapper men with hungry eyes and wide-open mouths dribbling at the sight of me. I like to flirt. I like to tease. Even the occasional striptease behind closed doors. What I don't particularly enjoy is being splattered with blood and viscera, or you know, being shot at. To each their own, I suppose. These are just not my kinks. But it could be worse."

"How is that?"

"We could be dead, or one of them could be alive to report back. The way I figure it, whether you've caught on or not, you have been driving to his house all this time. Subconsciously, you took in what I said about the money. We still have time. A small amount. Just enough to use to our advantage."

*He didn't do too bad, actually. He even changed it to the present, erroneously forgetting he started off in past tense. I honestly expected worse. Now he is all exhausted, clamoring for a break, mentally worn out from writing down a few sentences. Typical. One of those writers who hold themselves up to unrealistic standards. Expecting to wrench brilliancy from every goddamn sentence. Let him take his undeserved break while we continue.*

"Run where? You can't be this naïve. He will find us. If that's your plan you might as well pull over right now, take out your gun and blow your brains out. I will use it right after you."

"Sure you would."

"You don't trust me?"

"I don't trust anyone. Especially some broad."

"I could be your broad."

"If we get the money."

"If we get that money."

"You have it all planned out. Don't you?"

"Always have to have a plan. We are all out here looking for something. Figure out what it is and draft up a plan of how you are going to get it."

"That simple."

"That simple."

"Why'd'you do that, anyway? Behind his back."

"He's been around the block. And so have I. His kindness wasn't limitless. Sure, our relationship afforded me a certain lavish lifestyle. He constantly gave me money and never showed up empty-handed. But I wasn't the wife. I was the girl on the side. I like the security of knowing where I will wake up the next day without dependence on someone who might one day trade me in for a younger tart with a higher breast-line and pointier nipples. Until he came along, I didn't have any security, and I knew I never wanted to experience that again in case he tried to take it away. So, I sought and scavenged, always keeping my eyes out for an opportunity, much like the one fallen into our laps. I don't know about you, but I am tired of relying on others. I want to set myself up for the future."

"You want the perks without him around. And what makes me so different?"

"The money would be split equally, no obligations; if it works it works. And if it doesn't, we can move on. Go our separate ways financially secure."

"You are a natural deceiver. I don't know what to believe. I look at you and all I see is a facade. The revealing clothes you wear, your dyed hair, saucy demeanor, those large saucer eyes with the overload of makeup. You stand out. You want to stand out. But that's not you. That's not who you are. It's all an illusion, attempt to change your whole persona."

She fixes her stare out the passenger-side window. "Haven't you ever wanted to live your life as someone else? Just start over again?"

"I just haven't met anyone who went to all this trouble to get it."

"Then you never met anyone who wanted it enough."

"Alright, you got yourself a partner. But we won't be sharing a bed."

"You sure about that?"

"I can't sleep with anyone beside me."

"A man who likes his sleep. I can respect that."

*I didn't tell her right then and there that I wanted to be someone else as well. She would have laughed and told me to write us out of this mess. She was the real writer. She had it all down pat. And she was right. Some people just don't want it enough. I didn't. Otherwise, I would have never gotten in this hole. Writers write, the Ukrainian Canadian prick writing this story is writing, failing, sure, but he is trying, you can tell he wants it, to be up there with the greats. Tried more than I did, anyway. I just fell prey to my unstable mind and piling rejection letters.*

Michael pulls the car over. Keeps out of sight of the large mansion ahead.

"You will find him alone, waiting for his men to return. Don't underestimate him. Many others have, and none are around to boast about it. *Remember.* He keeps everything in the safe inside of his office. You will need the combination... unless you also moonlight as a safecracker when not living your dream job of a trigger man. With a man like this, I wouldn't rule out torture, he isn't one to blabber on and on without some prodding."

*A woman without limits. I was just as surprised as you are now, dear voracious readers/bookworms (burrowing deeper into the book, tunneling through the printed text, hanging onto every word) that she didn't carry around a pair of pliers in her purse for the job of teeth pulling, you know if torture shall arise, as it clearly has now. Alas, it was too late to brake, to break away. She had me where she wanted me, won over and enticed. I'd never be able to stay out of trouble with her around. It followed her wherever she went. And now she recruited me to disburse pain, collect money, nominal sympathy for the poor sucker about to get tortured and murdered. Murder was obligatory in a situation like this. Something I would not be able to avoid. I knew it as soon as I stepped out of the car. Desperate people in desperate situations with grim prospects, unless they commit to carrying out desperate deeds in hopes of large rewards.*

"Do you know how I knew you wanted the money?"

"Shoot."

"I thought that was your job."

"Smartass."

"When I first brought it up, and you didn't give me that uninterested look."

"So, it was my eyes that gave me away."

"Forget about your eyes. Come here. Come, give me a kiss."

"I love kissing wrong women, leading me toward a world of danger."

"Here."

She reaches inside her purse, perusing the interior until she has what she needs, a candy cane. She takes it out, her fingers waste no time unwrapping it. She inserts it in her slightly ajar mouth and starts to reduce the diameter down with her moist tongue, all wholesomeness withdrawn, lascivious behavior on full display for Michael's sole benefit. A spectator resuming his seat. When she has it exactly the way she wants it, she hands it back, thinned down on one end, made razor sharp by her luscious lips and tongue.

"For luck."

Inside the car, they talk, collaboratively, have a conspiratorial conversation, confer about things until both reach agreement exchanging nods before Michael gladly steps out of the smoke-filled crammed space greedily gobbling up fresh outdoor air—all this land, seemingly offering up widening opportunities, while the mind, the mental abacus that it is, rejects aesthetic pleasure and refrains from making painfully obvious observations, instead: zeroing in and narrowing probabilities until only one sure path remains. He turns to her. She smiles the eager smile of the unemployed and desperate, incisors on full display, life-sharpened, nicotine and coffee-stained sickly yellowed teeth from all the long days and late nights of plotting and scheming, momentarily caught by moonlight. Michael turns away, starts on foot toward the mansion in the distance, proprietor of a preoccupied mind, necessity for cash nipping him all over. Money, the stipulation for happiness. Her voice ringing in his ears, attuned to her serpentine words, nearing the mansion now, the big score, a simply irresistible opportunity to a pair of parasitic individuals.

*Wouldn't you know it? I think I imitated the pretentious bastard perfectly there. My gritty realism with his fanciful wordplay and melodramatic touches for the daytime soap opera crowd. Soon you won't be able to tell us apart. The corpse as you have probably guessed by now is of my ex-Boss. And believe me when I say he was one tough bastard. This wasn't some snotty teenager, this was a seasoned pro. Weathered, sure, but still with a few tricks up his sleeve. I hurled myself at him; he met me head-on, engaged me in an animalistic ritual. It was a beautiful sort of brutalization, a bewildering display of cruelty, a pair of uncaged snarling mongrels constantly colliding, gripping and grappling, wildly throwing punches, trying to land that fatal punch, smashing into furniture, their*

*bodies suffering, tortured, driven to the limits with
no time to recover, to catch their breath, swinging
and being swung on, fists hammering, mouths
spewing saliva and profanities, faces becoming
bloodier and bloodier and then a hand reaching,
inconspicuously procuring a candy cane of all
things, and with one swift movement the unsheathed
treat becomes a weapon, thrusting through the
eyeball and reaching the brain, a spike piercing and
penetrating, resulting in immediate brain death.
And there you have it, folks: a description of how
the once mighty fall from grace. A mafioso version
of Julius Caesar done in with a candy cane. And
here I am now, sitting on this crate waiting for my
better half, partner in crime, and something tells
me I won't have to wait long. Just a heads up, have
some patience folks, narrating in real time will be
a challenge, now that we are all caught up, with
the hard part out of the way, done away with the
murder and all and at last synched up to the present
time. But if you learned anything about me, is that
I am always up for a challenge.*

The cellar stairs squeak. Swift footsteps approach. Thunderbolt strikes. High heels on the stairs. Michael takes a last puff on his cigarette. He throws it down and crushes it with his scuffed leather shoe before he puts both of his hands inside his pants' pockets. Alessandra appears from the shadows, looking the part, the definition of desirability and eroticism. Her eyes pause on the dead body. Michael does not register shock or surprise in that impersonal gaze, just the absence of emotion.

"He was an obnoxious prick, but he seemed to know my pleasure points. Think you can figure them out by yourself? Don't think you can ask him now."

She moves closer, within reach. He touches her. She allows the touch, allows him to proceed. His hand on her leg, a hand constantly in motion. She responds, shuddering with pleasure, crumbling at the correctness of his touch.

"Warmer. Now go higher."

He moves his hand higher along her thigh. She gasps in ecstasy.

"Are you actually enjoying this, or have you consciously programmed yourself to like this?"

She banishes his hand from her thigh.

"Does this feel fake to you?"

She pushes him down. Straddles him. Floats above him, lost in her own erotic abandonment. He submits to her. Indulges. Admires her non-prudishness as she bares it all. An equestrian in her saddle. Two bodies in unified motion.

"Never figured you for the submissive sort," she says.

"You went to all this trouble. I might as well let you indulge. We can always switch later."

She bites his neck, breaks the skin, draws blood. They groan simultaneously. Clutch one another. Suffocate in their tightness. Magnets stuck together. He glides his hands across her drenched body. It glistens with sweat. Her sweat coats his hands. They both give themselves over, pursue their pleasures, satisfy their cravings.

"Did you get it?"

"What do you think?"

"I think you'd be a complete fool to have murdered him without getting that combination."

"The bag is right over there..." He nods in the direction of the bag. Her eyes follow his directional nod. The bag sits equidistant from the crate with his jacket and gun left on top and her purse thrown on the floor in the moment of heat next to a woodworking table.

"Full?"

"It's full. There's only one problem."

"There's not enough in there for two."

"There isn't."

"Which only means..."

"...which only means that only one of us is walking out of here alive."

She breaks away, sprints toward her purse, starts to fiendishly search inside. Michael cocks the gun. The sound startles her, makes her stop her frenzied search.

"I never carry just one gun. Don't you

remember from the hotel? A small caliber weapon fits a pants pocket just as well as a jacket without drawing any attention to itself. Always assume a man with a second gun has a third." He pulls his pants up. "Lay the gun down."

She retrieves Michael's other small caliber weapon from her purse and reluctantly lays it down on a table next to her.

"You are beautiful but sadly conniving to the point where trust is out of the question."

"You are the one with the gun. I am unarmed. Naked. There's little to fear."

"I fear the gossip. A witness to a murder talking to law enforcement in the near future. That mouth of yours tends to flap uncontrollably."

"Well, make it stop, lover. Give it a kiss."

Michael decides to take her up on her proposition. He raises his gun, aims it directly at her chest, walks over and kisses her passionately.

"God, you are beautiful."

"Obviously not beautiful enough for you to keep alive."

"Sadly, no."

*Aghhhhhh...*

[Shut up! You are ruining the scene with your agonizing screaming. The audience needs to know what happened.]

Alessandra reaches toward the nape of her neck, retrieving a taped down replacement razor blade, concealed by her long lustrous hair. Straightaway she slashes through the air and Michael's neck. He loses his balance, stumbles around, clutching at his throat, unable to stop the bleeding, dripping blood all over the floor, resisting against death's encroachment. She watches him, unaffected by his suffering. He sits down on the crate to keep from falling, ending the mad dashing about the space. The restlessness is now only inside of his mind, the restlessness of a man nearing his end.

"Isn't your darling absolutely deplorable? You must despise her. Coaxing you into a trap like that. Do you want a handkerchief? You are gushing all over your recently procured, former employer's spotless starched-white dress shirt. Or how about a glass of cold water? Something to help clear that lump in your throat."

Her savage snickering fills the cellar. She picks his jacket up from the crate, reaches inside, takes out a crumpled pack of cigarettes and lights one up. He continues to bleed profusely. She takes a long draw on his cigarette, blows out a few smoke rings toward his face, the rings expanding until they dissolve upon facial impact, adding another layer of pain to his contorted face.

"Men and their inability to turn down any form of sex." She shakes her head. "I spread my legs and here comes my knight in shinning armor. I offer a kiss and here he is again, galloping at full speed with a hard on instead of a lance or a sword, wanting to play his little power games and exchange saliva, bacteria and mucus. How pathetic and sad. Don't you understand your current predicament was foreseeable. You just didn't look hard enough, didn't pay close enough attention to the warning signs. You aren't cut out for this. That's the bottom line. The stakes are higher, there are no second prizes for the runners-up. You don't get your little ribbon. You are lucky if you walk away with your life. And clearly, you haven't been that lucky. Self-control and a bit of street smarts is all it takes to navigate this shapeless world. Slapping women and pointing guns will only get you so far. You should have known better. You should have learned along the way. Got to know yourself a bit better. Understood who you were and where you belonged. I understood the moment I saw you. I can always tell a mark a mile away."

Alessandra picks up the bag. Halfway up the stairs, she shuts the lights on the doubled over prisoner, plunging him with a single switch, a single brushstroke into black bituminous all eclipsing darkness. And she is gone. The red-haired, scheming temptress from hell. What attracted Michael to her, attracted many men

in his position now. She would have got you **too,**
dear reader. Her strength. Her intelligence. Her
sexual allure. You are in denial if you are under
the impression she could ever love anyone except
herself. Ruthless and deadly. Temptress **par**
excellence.

 

*I didn't see this coming.*

[But I did.]

*Oh, it's you, you sniveling bastard. You have
discovered my additions, followed the trail of my
internal thoughts.*

[I did. That is why I am letting you bleed
out now. You could have had the money. But you
got greedy. Backstabbing. This is punishment for
your tempering.]

*I hate your ending.*

[Of course, you do. I am sure you had a
better one planned.]

*After I had gotten the money and killed that
long-legged bimbo, I would have driven away with
one last thought on my mind. A flashback scene that*

*repeats itself constantly in my life. Reminding me not to forget it, to let it slip away. A scene I always questioned. Taking place during my drunkard days. Fittingly, a scene that supposedly happened in a bar.*

[I know the one you are talking about. It's on the cutting-room floor.]

*You bastard! It would have been perfect.*

[Possibly, but we'll never know now.]

*Do me a favor. Type it out just for me. For my eyes only. The reader doesn't have to see it. I know I messed up, that's just who I am, a fuck-up. Grant a dying man his dying wish—I will be eternally grateful.*

[What does it matter now. Have it your way, I'll even do it in your style.]

*Mix our styles.*

Michael enters a Sin City pavilion attached to the main building. A member-only joint. A place where you can freely move around without worrying about law enforcement and scores that need to be settled in a public place—mob enforcers following the ordinance of the higher ups, sending their calling-card murder messages.

He takes a seat at the counter, striking in his expensive new suit. The bartender nods. He knows Michael, many others do as well. A glass of whisky magically appears before him, sparkling invitingly under all the lights. Before he has time to raise it to his thirsty lips, he feels a hand on his shoulder. Michael turns, suddenly face to face with his scantily dressed ex-wife, hardly recognisable behind all the caked-on makeup and the large serving tray in her hands. She uncertainly looks him over.

"Michael?"

"Last time I checked."

"Not exactly what I hoped you would say."

"You work here?"

"I do."

"Well, you should know better than to talk about hope. Hope comes here to die." He could tell she felt the brunt of his condescending tone. "Looks like a reversal of fortune from where I am sitting."

"Spiteful. You've probably been waiting for this day for a long while now. So, go on you fucker, rub it in."

He looks over her shoulder: a gentleman at the end of the bar is attempting to get her attention. "We will have to continue this some other time. You got a customer to service."

Her complexion becomes frighteningly pale. He finishes his drink in one gulp, standing up, a self-satisfying smile playing across his lips. With his back to the only woman he ever loved, the self-proclaimed victor walks away.

*Did this really happen? Did I really hurt her a second time around? Threw away my only chance for redemption? For happiness?*

[I don't know. Only you would know the answer to this. All I know is that you have never walked away 'victoriously' from anything in your life. And now its time for you to die and for me to type The End, concluding this cautionary tale which should make the readers feel better about their own lives, those nice and boring and very safe lives.]

# THE MOTEL

*Y*OU *WOULD BE HARD-PRESSED to find a more remote place on any map.* This passing thought raced through the busy mind of Timothy Price as he looked around the savage desert wasteland. He found the bareness of it all unsettling. Getting lost out here meant handfuls of sand before a drop of water would ever turn up—a slow, torturous death.

Timothy rested his elbows on the hot aluminum

handrail of the motel's second-story corridor. He shielded his eyes to see if he could spot anything else around, only to return to the single road by which he had arrived. Forking just once, Timothy had taken a left turn to reach this wonderful architectural landmark in the Nevada desert.

The motel stood dominantly over an inexhaustible expanse of sand. A raw deal, perhaps, but a motel superimposed in the middle of nowhere provided a great deal of anonymity to travelers whose lives depended on it.

Timothy hated that he was such a traveler. He had often landed in hot water, knew what being preyed upon was like. Except this was a few notches above the usual, involving an actual hideaway, with deadly consequences if he was caught. He was never the type to delude himself about his faults, never the type to not be able to name them if pressed on the spot about them. The only answers he fumbled were usually to the hard questions asked by toughs he encountered along the way. And those were always about money.

Borrowing money, how much was owed and repayment of that money. This partly explained how he ended up here, but did it matter in the end? The bottom line was he was here now, and he got here due to the addictive nature of his character and the fact that he owed much money to those very same toughs. And instead of the more sensible solution of actually paying back the money, Timothy decided to skip town.

He wiped his forehead with the back of his sleeve, irritated and utterly defeated—painstakingly trying to rouse his unresponsive mind.

Timothy consulted his watch—it was just after 6 PM. His hands plunged deep into the pockets of his dirty corduroys and fished out a pack of Camels. He dropped his head forward over his cupped hands, protecting the flame of a sparked match. As he raised his head, his peripheral vision intercepted something in the distance approaching at high velocity.

Sweat began to trickle down the back of his shirt. He stood stone still.

If it were daytime, he could attribute it to a mirage, but since it was evening all he could do was convince himself it was the product of a tired mind and the merciless heat. He tried in vain, tried his hardest to be a sceptic even when facing irrefutable truth, not daring to look away, continuing to fixedly stare at the swiftly approaching object. It was hard to make out any details at first, but as the object neared it caught the fading light, allowing Timothy to identify the emerging apparition as a classic '72 Corvette.

His quivering lips dislodged the cigarette firmly held in place just seconds ago. "*It's just a car,*" he kept repeating. It would not mean a thing to anyone but him...

He drew back, hyperventilating and trying to gulp at the stale evening air. His heartbeat reached a sickening crescendo while his shaky hands fumbled for the rusted doorknob of his room.

Once inside, he automatically pulled the tattered and faded curtain across the smudged window next to the door. He snapped the lock in place and connected the chain to the track, knowing full well it would not withstand the slightest pressure.

With his back against the door and his shoulders slumped, he felt helpless—an animal caged in a tiny room. The door did not even have a peephole. All he could do was stand there and listen for anything that would break the silence.

Minutes passed, nothing happened.

Timothy was not so easily dissuaded and kept on listening. Fear makes a person stubborn—especially when their life hangs in the balance. Finally, becoming decidedly impatient, he dropped to his knees and sprawled across the stained, foul-smelling carpet. He peered along the gap created by the door and held back a startled shout when he observed a pair of dark shoes on the other side.

Next to the stranger's shoes was Timothy's burning cigarette, which he had forgotten in his haste to hide inside his room. With disbelief, he watched as the red ember of the cigarette lifted from the floor and disappeared from his restricted vantage point. The cigarette never did reappear, nor had Timothy seen the hand that surely retrieved it from the ground. The man must be puffing on the cigarette, Timothy thought, and wearing black leather gloves that blended with the darkness of the evening.

He finally heard the man walk away, heard sounds in the room next door, and not long after Timothy's eyelids grew heavy, twitched, and drooped shut. He felt twice his age, worn out by sheer stress.

*They have found me. No great surprise there. It was always just a matter of time.*


Timothy awoke with his teeth clenched around the worn-out carpet. Dissatisfied with his polypropylene breakfast, he quickly spat it out. His back was stiff from sleeping on the floor. Then again, it was always stiff.

He stood up with all the briskness he could

muster and clumsily made his way to the bathroom sink where he vigorously scrubbed his face
and rinsed out his mouth.

Slowly coming to, he recounted the final
harrowing minutes of last night with increasing
uneasiness. Fear once again doused him like the
most pungent of colognes, fully rousing him. He
began to pace the length of the room with great
deliberation, obsessively darting his eyes between
the front door and the cheap wall clock with its
hope-crushing hands pronouncing nothing but
continuing despair.

His life depended on a letter. Its contents
would tell him if she were safe and if they could
still rendezvous at the agreed location. He had to
have it. However, for him to grab hold of it, he
had to travel down to the manager's office on the
first floor.

This, of course, meant leaving his room
unoccupied with all his meager but valuable
possessions.

Moreover, if his next-door neighbor happened

to be an assassin sent to kill him, he did not want to walk into a trap upon his return to the room.

An idea came to him. He put on his jacket and tore a loose thread from one of the sleeves. He licked the palm of his hand as well as the thread and left it there, glued to his palm, obscured from the sight of any prying eyes.

Timothy walked out into the sunshine and started to lock the door, covertly pressing the palm of his hand underneath the handle, positioning the thread there with one end sticking to the door and the other to the frame.

He descended the exterior stairs two at a time, clutching the rail for support and attentively listening for any noise.

Everything seemed calm.

The manager's office was the last door on the far left. He purposefully continued toward his goal, trying hard to ignore the distance, but something made him halt mid stride—the '72 Corvette. Parked directly in front of the manager's office, it had been blocked from the panoramic view of the second floor by the protruding awning.

His body tensed and his feet felt rooted to the walkway while his mind spun out of control with violent thoughts.

*Was the stranger inside the office now?*

Timothy knew that uncertainty feeds paranoia and fear. He also knew he had to dispel it. Summoning a fictitious surge of adrenaline, he yanked the door wide open and darted inside the office.

The office was a mess, littered with loose papers and junk stacked in pyramidal shapes, with no shortage of cobwebs and general filth that goes along with a place that has not seen a cleaning in at least a decade. There was also a sickening stench that lingered in the air and slowly crept up Timothy's nostrils. Covering his nose and mouth, he focused upon the wall-sized-unit behind the empty concierge's desk with its numerous identical boxes.

There was no letter in 10-B.

He had told her ahead of time where he would

be. He thought it would certainly reach here by now. That is, unless something went wrong...

"Can I be of service, monsieur?"

She startled him; he had overlooked her presence amidst the chaos. But there she was in her receptionist attire in the far corner, making her way toward the desk.

The surprise left Timothy temporarily mute. Noticing his lack of initiative, she addressed him cordially in slightly accented French, "I hope you found your room to your liking. It's fortunate that the gentleman who booked it in advance never checked in to claim it."

"You mean to tell me..."

"Yes, monsieur. It was the last room to get booked, if that's your question. We have a full booking at the motel."

"But I haven't seen anyone else around..."

"The customers like their privacy, monsieur. Naturally, we do everything in our power to meet their needs."

*Naturally*, thought Timothy. An array of

subversive lodgers staying at a motel with a reputation for tucking away murderers, gamblers, and other vagrants. Fate has a dark and twisted sense of humor. The only room that he was able to book had a last-minute cancellation. Cancellation by a much-wanted party, apparently, judging by the personage situated right next door.

This truly was the worst case of mistaken identity. It is not him that the man next door wanted. However, what could he do? He could not just knock on the door and explain all this to the potential murderer of the man who never showed up to claim his room. It was all a stretch, a jump to conclusions, but Timothy trusted his intuition, plus it simply added up. If they were business partners, had business to attend to, the stranger would have knocked on the door instead of threateningly standing outside the door without even considering knocking, wanting his presence kept a secret.

It was imperative at this point to return to the room and think it all over.

Timothy exchanged a weak goodbye with the woman and hurried back. Even with this new development he had a presentiment that something awful was going to happen before the day was up. A gambler always knows. As long as he could remember, Timothy had referred to it as, "Gambler's intuition." When the powers that be conspired against the player, delivering a storm of bad luck, too many terrible coincidences occurring not to know you are in the eye of a bad streak, and while it will eventually break or so goes the "Gambler's fallacy," it has to fulfill its purpose, and the player must decide whether to weather the storm or call it a day.

With this raging weather, these torrential thoughts, Timothy reached his room, so lost in his own mental downpour that he almost opened the door without checking for the piece of thread. He looked closely, but it was not there.

The stranger's timing was immaculate—able to lock pick his way inside the room and have a look around in a short amount of time.

Timothy opened the door with a trembling hand. He knew his face must be pale from unadulterated terror. He also knew he had to check the room. What if the stranger was still inside? Unable to get out in time. Now silently waiting. Hidden in the closet or underneath the bed. Biding his time. In his fear-stricken state, with his heart beating furiously and hands trembling uncontrollably, Timothy somehow mustered enough courage to check both hiding places, finding no other occupant except himself and the terrible tentacles of terror suffocating all life from him.

The room began to spin—his spellbound eyes traveling with the rotation until they finally settled on a picture of a yacht. It was the only picture in the room. One he had noticed earlier. A picture which was now slightly *askew*. Hung on the wall he shared with...

Timothy felt the weight and the futility of the situation. This was not good. Not good at all. A doomsday pronouncement was clearly upon him. He felt nervous, skittish, bathing in his own sweat unaided by this stiflingly hot room.

His mind brimmed with the worst possible thoughts; the type of thoughts that tend to disfigure perception and cloud over clear-headedness. He had gotten himself mixed up, entangled in a situation with absolutely no ability to call the shots.

Timothy had to do the unfathomable. He knew this, but he could not allow the idea to take its rightful place in his mind. He had to examine the back of the picture. To cross the room without raising suspicion: freedom of movement, something we take for granted every day. Timothy scanned the room. A desperate darting around his detention cell.

He stopped his search at his feet. His heavy leather shoes were utilitarian by all definitions, but were thick-soled, hindering him all the same. Sure, the room had wall-to-wall carpet, but the floor also had a squeak, he remembered. But where exactly? *God, what if he stepped on that godforsaken deficient noisy floorboard?*

Slowly, very slowly he started to bend his body forward with that knowledge never leaving his mind. Desperation emboldens people. It makes them fight and scratch for their dear life. They do not want to let go. Timothy was one of those. The not wanting to let go types. He wanted time, his time, as much time as he could get his hands on, fit in his grubby degenerate gambler's hands, and carry off with him. So, he went to the task at hand and began to untie his shoelaces.

Thankfully, the shoes untied rather easily, and he could slip his feet out after unfastening the laces a bit. His feet now free of their shackles, the day's perspiration able to roam the small quarters, a pungent aroma from his formerly incubated sweltering feet striking the inside of Timothy's defenseless nose, making him wince. But the shoes were off. This was not insignificant in any sense. A victory indeed, no matter how small. He smiled for the first time since he got here—a chance this all will not end in disaster.

Timothy set the shoes down next to the bed.

He fetched his travel bag resting on the one side and carefully undid the zipper. Inside the bag, he located a pair of tight leather gloves. He put these on to help with the slickness of his hands. The material quickly absorbed the moisture. He clasped his hands together, interlacing the fingers to help the absorption process along.

Now he had to climb the unassailable mountain—a figure of speech that never rang truer to Timothy than at this decisive moment. He straightened up, forfeiting his half-bent position over the bed.

Timothy took his first step forward. The wheels started to revolve; events set in motion. He could not stop now. There was no time to stand still and reflect on this one slight step forward. He had to follow it with more such steps and time was surely running out.

He resumed his tiptoeing, trying to tread lighter, dedicated to one, and only one task at hand, putting faith in each step, trusting that this forward movement would ameliorate the predicament he was in.

When he reached the picture, he knew this was the moment of absolute truth. The moment which would reveal to him whether he could genuinely face his demonic and thirsting fears and stand up to them, because to go back, there was not anywhere to go back to. To go back meant cellular death, the expiration of the flesh, a freshly dug-up grave reserved just for him to join the long list of dearly departed and soon forgotten individuals who once inhabited this earth.

He lifted the frame, thinking about his own placement in the world of the living things. On the back of this cheap, enlarged and framed photograph, a tiny jet-black device greeted him, the kind often described in dime-store spy thrillers, not that Timothy was ever a keen reader...

A listening device. A bug.

His worst-case scenario involving unlawful entry successfully fulfilled.

He had no doubts about what the stranger was doing at this very moment: conducting audio surveillance with this microscopic microphone, capturing and recording sound, dissecting and scrutinizing high spikes in volume.

Timothy thanked named and unnamed gods for the fact the picture frame had a string instead of a  chain which would have scraped against the nail on which it hung, giving him away the moment he lifted the frame.

He knew he would have to remove the listening device. It was the only way. The listening device itself was power. It immured him to his smallish room, putting him at a great disadvantage, unable to leave without his captor knowing it.

Grasping the picture firmly with his gloved hands, he carefully moved toward the bed. This meant traversing the uneven terrain of the worn-out carpet—with areas exposing the squeaky rotting wood underneath. He feared the fateful creaking misstep, or worse, a toe-catching fall, the unmistakable thud.

Halfway across he realized he was not breathing. What if he passed out? He took a step. No creak. Then another. Silence. His lungs ached for air.

Six excruciating steps later, safely at the bed, lightheaded but able to breathe again, he placed the picture face down, the device dead center in the back of the picture like a hidden message, authorial inscription, a signature belonging to the sadistic surveillance expert on the other side of the wall. He knew he must hurry. With his right hand he reached out, trembling from the massiveness of the moment—everything surging inside of him. He tugged. The device did not budge. Fear seized hold of him. His face resembled a death mask. Sweat droplets fell from his forehead to the semi-carpeted floor.

He took a deep breath, trying his best to eradicate all negative thoughts, and reached for the device once more. This time he was able to carefully pry it away from the picture-backing, taking a moment to hold it between his gloved fingers in reverence—an aesthete admiring his priceless acquisition.

Now that Timothy had the object, he realized he never carefully thought-out all the details beforehand, such as what he would do with it once he had it in his hands. The story of his life: the doubting mentality of a self-defeatist. He would just have to wing it, improvise on the spot, an actor following instinct rather than script.

Through the process of disqualification, he settled for the bed, unblemished and unslept in as of the night before last. He placed the device in the middle and carefully smothered it with layers of bedding. Surely the only thing it would transmit now would be utter silence.

Now, with the device entombed in layers of cotton and polyester, Timothy, no longer worried about detection of his movements, returned the picture to its rightful place on the wall—*Bugger off you bug, he thought.*

As the string pulled taut, stretching itself to the limit against the rickety, corroded nail, he happened to recall his gambling past—hopefully, the past if he learns a lesson from this experience and lives to abide by a new way of living—where this current predicament mirrors precisely the moment in the game that propels most degenerate gamblers to continue to gamble. The moment when a lousy streak turns winning, turning the tables around on the croupier as a glimmer of hope shines through. Brief as it may be.

Timothy suddenly felt weak and collapsed on the bed, dehydrated, exhausted and starving. The room started to revolve. He felt as if he were in an oneiric state where everything he knew as being solid and dependable abruptly became a caricature of its former self. Nothing was durable, crumbling at a mere touch. There was a hollowness and collapsibility to everything, nothing had any soundness left to it, no longer check-marked and approved, classifiable as trustworthy, imperishability was a thing of the past. And so was he. Collapsing under pressure. Allowing darkness to reign.

*

Timothy stirred. His facial muscles twitched. He felt the overnight settled soreness that had spread throughout his body. His eyelids seemed stuck together. He fluttered them repeatedly until he was able to keep them open. Timothy knew he had fainted. He had suffered these fainting spells for a long time now due to his hereditary heightened stress reactions, and whenever he awoke for the inescapable return to the present, reality always seemed intrusive, especially after an episode of deliberate forgetfulness.

For the second time now, he found himself in a contorted position on the floor, splayed out awkwardly in the dark. He slowly raised himself up. A splitting headache besieged the cupola on top of his shoulders and neck. He felt terribly parched, and while the combination of the excruciating pain and the insatiable thirst were undoubtedly horrific, the incoming, invading thoughts were even worse. He shook his head from side to side, desperate to rid himself of them.

During this side-to-side headshake, indistinct

sounds from the great outdoors reached Timothy's ears. He stopped, stood, grabbed the closest wall to steady himself, and made his way over to the window. A bright light framed the door.

The involuntary tremble was back in his hands. With deliberate slowness, trying fruitlessly to escape the inevitable, he moved the curtain to one side, confronting a set of headlights. Someone else had arrived at the party.

He lost sight of the car once it travelled underneath the awning to park. Timothy had to rely on his ears now. First, he heard the declarative statement of a car door forcefully slammed shut. Then, the newcomer's quick footsteps leading up to the motel. A door opened and closed somewhere on the first floor. *Must be the manager's office*, thought Timothy. His heart began to pound—an erratic, quickening beat. His hopes of escape wilting.

The downstairs door *clanged* again, opened-and-shut by a robust hand unafraid of drawing attention to itself. A *jingling* sound followed. Had to be multiple keys on a key ring. Then, more footsteps, intensifying as the person neared. *I should run, I should do it now,* thought Timothy, but something held him back. He allowed the moment of hesitation to overrule all else and was now forced to endure the ever familiar feeling a person gets before their space is invaded. A moment of complete powerlessness.

Footfalls now sounded on the stairs. A confident, quickened pace. Timothy tried to swallow the lump in his throat, but there was not enough saliva for even that—an acidic taste permeated his entire mouth, making him nauseous the more he tasted it.

He looked around the room until his eyes returned to the front door. A whole other world awaited him beyond that locked door, if he could only open it. But he knew he would not even try. All he could do was stand and wait, consumed by every sound that reached him, by the nearby footfalls and all the other echoings in the night.

The footsteps finally came to a halt. There

was a change. All the other noises faded as if in preparation for the prophesied knock, which never did befall the brittle door. Just silence. Unnerving seemingly never-ending silence.

Timothy could not stay in the dark for long, and not learning his lesson the first time around, resorted to flattening himself on the floor once more, peering through the gap just in time to see what he could only describe as a sudden violent flash. Something described as a "golden splendor" in those chippie espionage paperbacks, his continual reference guide to all things above the low-level criminal activity he was used to. *A bullet. It had to be a bullet!* He could have sworn he even heard the muffled scream when the bullet pierced the soft tissue of the human body.

He did not have all the answers, he could only figure out certain parts, but the end result was clear enough. The matter of the murder itself was not a very complicated affair: it has taken place and produced a body (reasonable guess: the car-door-slamming newcomer) which was now being dragged away by the next-door neighbor.

The weapon, the originator of the "golden splendor," gave his neighbor god-like omnipotence. But even without the weapon, Timothy was no match for the man. He only had one course of action available now. To run as fast and as far as he could. Luckily, the disposal of the body allotted time for this final move, the betting of all the chips. All in, with everything to lose, including his life.

Timothy pivoted and directed his gaze toward the bathroom window. It transfixed him. Beyond the low-grade wooden frame still holding the smeared glass in place, was freedom. He could feel how tangible it truly was. Beyond that smudged window was a sand-swept terrain, a hidden Biblical desert, ready to welcome him, a foolish man, a captive saved by the immeasurable sand that resembles the sea.

Yes, this was the only definitive way. The front door was not. Not an option. Not even up for consideration. His mind raced forward, a tireless abacist calculating probabilities. *Would he fit?* It did not look advisable at all, especially for someone who feared heights.

Timothy approached the window, a hybrid of emotional states, hesitant yet hard-boiled. Looking for resolve, yet terrified of not finding it in the last available place. He tried the window; it did not budge. He tried it again. On the second attempt it yielded easily enough, and as he stared down from the highest point of the motel (excluding that of the rooftop) he could not help but wonder about the horrible, severe fall which awaited anyone unlucky enough to lose one's grip and balance. A toss-up between paralysis and a slow, agonizing death.

He was fully betting on himself to be the recipient of such a death, or paralysis. Either one was a distinctive possibility, if not a probability. *A fitting end to a subterranean life spent without a single crowning achievement,* Timothy thought, hardly a life worth envying. Some would even call this self-inflicted redemption, a mercy killing, a way to set things right.

Timothy knew he would try regardless, even if the odds had been entirely against him since his arrival here. Most people find it worthwhile to try to salvage something, up to a certain point, before throwing in the towel and checking out, resigning to their unchangeable fate and living out the rest of their lives with their heads down and hopes crushed. Few lucky ones succeed at beating the odds, winning the fight against that unwavering belief of some in the predetermined destiny of their lives and gain the ability to manufacture their own life anew.

He turned away from the window. Prolonged staring would not change the possible outcomes of his self-proposed great escape. He shook his head and walked back into the room. Everything would have to happen with exactitude and precision. One does not just scale down the side of a motel without preparation beforehand.

Not to mention that thirty feet of rope was not included with the fresh linens and toilet articles. He would have to improvise, most likely settle for the bedsheets, making sure to twist them all the way around until they resembled a cable of cotton strong enough to hold his weight. Once he touched solid ground, he would have to make his way to his car completely unobserved. Making it not only a great, but a brazen escape, to say the least.

The preparations took time. A half hour vanished. Forfeited time, irreclaimable minutes and seconds Timothy would not be getting back, but miraculously the perfect amount for him to construct his makeshift rope. He knew he had pushed his luck. That the Reckoning Hour was now upon him. His self-indulgence for survival had landed him on the ledge of the motel's second-story window, his hands gripping the twisted bedsheets. He looked down at concrete and sand. The height was the barrier. *Surely the knots would fail.* One could call this an individual's protestation in the face of a calamitous set of circumstances, ones surely to result in death. Although, he might live to tell the tale.

A wave of numbness suddenly seeped through him. Timothy's mind was now at a standstill. No profundity of original ideas, not the flimsiest impression of a thought. *How could this be?* He looked back at the room, the door. Then he looked back down again. It should have been an uneventful stay. It did not work out according to plan. *Nothing ever does anyway.*

He took a step forward. His foot never connected with a solid surface, and Timothy plunged ahead. His free fall lasted only seconds before his makeshift rope did its part, propelling him back toward the side of the building, making him collide violently with the edifice. His left shoulder bore the brunt of the impact, which stiffened up his entire body.

Timothy did not dare let go, knowing full well his hard landing would create too much disturbance. He persisted, carrying on, enduring incredible pain with his hands clutching desperately to the rope, descending slowly toward solid ground.

And then it happened, just as it had happened before—everything became nebulous. And he knew that his hands would let go. Knew all too well that he would plummet below, unconscious by this point, finally impacting with the ground; the culprit responsible for putting a stop to his fall.

*"Where am I? What is this? It's you... Look... It's all been a big misunderstanding. I know I am not the one you want. What could you possibly want with me? I am no one. No one of any importance. No one to catch the attention of someone of your stature. It's all been a piece of bad luck. A terrible coincidence. I've never even seen your face. I can't even see it now with the sun positioned behind you. I don't even know your name. Or the reason you are here. I know absolutely nothing about your business*

*here. I was just frightened. That's why I ran. I am easily spooked. I heard a noise that made my blood run cold. I thought someone was lock-picking my door, trying to rob me in the middle of the night. That's all it was. I swear. I never saw a thing. I just heard something that frightened me. You have to believe me. Please put that shovel down. I beg you. You don't need to do this. I am an innocent bystander. There is no need for this. You have no reason to eliminate me. To bury me out here in the middle of the desert. I saw nothing. I am telling you, I just got spooked. A loud noise startled me, that's all. Just rotten luck. That's all this is. Who am I? I am no one. A degenerate gambler evading loan sharks holed up in a run-down motel in the middle of the desert. You see, absolutely no one to worry about. I am so tiny in the grand scheme of things. A man who spent his whole life evading. Evading responsibilities and creditors. Always on the run from someone I owed money to. But I know you aren't one of them. I know it's not a case of that. I am just a parasite. A degenerate on the move.*

*Been running my whole life. Had an early start in childhood before the other kids and never stopped. You have no idea how exhausting it is. To never be able to catch your breath. Constantly looking over your shoulder. Please put that shovel down. It's all just one big mistake. I am not the one you want. How can I be? I am no one. A great big nothing. A roach under the floorboards of this motel. Aren't you tired of shovelling? Put the shovel down for a moment. Take a break. You are right, my teeth are chattering. And yes, I am talking excessively. I can't help it. I am anxious about being buried alive in the middle of this godforsaken desert. Forgive me. But no, I don't think anything can alleviate this stress unless you stop filling this hole. What's this you've thrown. I didn't mean to imply at me. I am sorry I can't seem to find the right words. A book? But how can this help? Read the title? You want me to read the title. A Spy's Espionage Story... this can't be. It can't be the same book. That's the book I kept thinking about the whole time. Trying to remember the name. I don't understand. How can you possibly have this book? A thrift store on the way to the airport? A dollar? What do you mean, it makes sense? Nothing makes sense about this. Fate? This can't be fated. How could I have ever considered the possibility this was meant to happen? I am not clairvoyant. I am not a fortune teller. Stop. Please stop shovelling! No. I can't just stop talking. If I stop I... That's easy for you to say. Resign sure. Just resign to my fate. It's inescapable. I have no control over what is happening to me. That's easy for you to say! How can this be... this can't be right? An infinitude of possibilities all converging to the same outcome. You are insane. A madman! Each and every time... The exact same outcome? You believe in this? I am not the person you want. Don't you get it?! I am an innocent bystander. Our paths weren't always going to cross. That's just not true. Insanity... what insanity. What roles... what script to follow? I have no idea what you are talking about. Prefigured by someone else for us? By whom?! God? You are saying you are the killer; other man was the intended target, and I was the innocent bystander? I have no idea what you are talking about. Killed whom? I hadn't even seen anyone else here except the woman tending the front desk. Stop shoveling. Just stop, will you? For godsakes stop! And stop telling me to resign to my fate. It doesn't add up, don't you see? It's erroneous. An erasure of everything that has led up to this moment. No, I don't think it fits. Stop. Just stop! This can't be real. I must have fallen and died. That's it, I just never made it down that makeshift rope. I let go, which isn't surprising with my weak upper body strength. I let go, and I fell down. Either killed on impact or sprawled on the concrete unconscious, bleeding out from a head wound. This can't be real. This cannot be my reality. This is something else. I fell asleep. Maybe I never even left the last casino, fallen over the slot machine, drunk, still clutching the handle. What do you mean prepare? Prepare for what? The death of hope? Please don't. The sand is already up to my neck. Please have mercy on me. Spare me. Please... I am begging you!"*

# MY HAUNTED LIFE

# THE CHARACTERS

MAN – A man in his 40s.
WOMAN – A woman in her 40s.

# THE SCENE

*A moving car.*

MAN: What do you see when you close your eyes?

WOMAN: Nothing. (*Pause.*) What about you?

MAN: I can't close my eyes. I'm driving.

WOMAN: Just for a second...

MAN: I see you.

WOMAN: That's because you were just looking at me.

MAN: No, I wasn't. I was looking at the road. (*Pause.*) I wish every time I closed my eyes... I could see you without other imagery intruding. To close my eyes, and for only you to be there. Every single time.

WOMAN: Now now. Don't be greedy. Not

seeing me every time, all the time, gives you a chance to miss me. And then when we finally see each other it's...

MAN: Ignited gunpowder.

WOMAN: Fireworks.

MAN: You know, when we first met, I would watch you sleep for hours on end. I'd hardly blink, just stare at your rising and falling chest.

WOMAN: Why were you afraid to blink?

MAN: I was afraid that if I closed my eyes, by the time I opened them again, you would be gone.

WOMAN: Not the type to usually vanish without saying goodbye.

MAN: I couldn't imagine my life without you.

WOMAN: Try. What would you do?

MAN: I think I would live among my memories of you, opt for make-believe. Nostalgia, lost in the immediacy of the transpired moment.

A permanent resident in a fantasy world I've created.

WOMAN: Sounds like the perfect opportunity to reflect on your life. Your past, present, perhaps even future.

MAN: There could never be thoughts about the future without you around. I would be like a patient on life support suddenly unplugged, just those seven minutes of reminiscences about you, and then I would fade away.

WOMAN: If you had to pick only one memory, which one would it be?

MAN: You aren't making it easy, are you?

WOMAN: Where would the fun be in that?

MAN: It'd have to be your last birthday. When we splurged on a weekend we really couldn't afford to stay at that fancy hotel spa place.

WOMAN: Great sex, but even better food.

(*He throws his hands up in protest of culinary*

*wonders beating out sexual escapades.*)

But why that day? What made it so special to you?

MAN: Just the fact that I have never seen you so relaxed. You were calm and vulnerable. You really opened up to me.

WOMAN: And that's when you felt comfortable enough to tell me you loved me.

MAN: The setting was perfect and the moment too precious to waste. It's been on my mind for a while. I felt a great relief and a great warmth when I uttered those words for the very first time.

WOMAN: And you haven't stopped saying them since.

MAN: I never want to stop saying them. I love saying them.

WOMAN: And what about the worst memory? The one that haunts you the most.

MAN: Should I even have one of those?

WOMAN: Stop being cheeky. Every couple has one of those. And it's probably the one you replay the most in your mind.

MAN: Even over the best one?

WOMAN: We always tend to remember the negative memories more. Don't ask me why, I am not a psychologist, but there's something about them; they stick out and get stuck in our memory banks.

MAN: (*He frowns.*) Well, there is one...

WOMAN: I knew there was. You just don't like to talk about it.

MAN: I don't. It hurts too much to say it out loud.

WOMAN: Well, now is your chance to tell me.

MAN: Do you remember when we both developed that obsession, that preoccupation with the paranormal?

WOMAN: Yes. We can thank reality television for that.

MAN: Right. And we decided to take a road trip to Bodie.

WOMAN: Bodie...

MAN: Remember that abandoned mining town.

WOMAN: I do. Yes. I remember now. Strange, I had forgotten about that.

MAN: I wish I could.

WOMAN: Keep going, help me with my recollection.

MAN: We got there and...

WOMAN: It turned out to be exactly as advertised. Not a soul around.

MAN: If you keep interrupting, I won't bother to tell it at all.

WOMAN: Go ahead. I will be the definition of quietude.

MAN: We got there. And it was abandoned, just like you said. But that wasn't it. There was something else. Something I hadn't counted on. The silence of the place. How sharp it was. Crawling under your skin. A silence with a set of eyes, never letting you get out of its sight. Just us surrounded by this silence and the deathly stillness. I told you to wait in the car while I looked around.

WOMAN: I didn't listen.

MAN: Of course, you didn't. You are too fiercely independent for something like that.

WOMAN: I got scared of being alone in the car. I also didn't want you out there by yourself.

MAN: Whatever happened to staying quiet and listening?

WOMAN: Too fiercely independent, remember? A real problem when it comes to compliance.

MAN: (*Sighs.*) I remember. (*Pause.*) So we both left the car and went to explore. We ended up at this building. It was larger than all the rest. My mind raced standing next to it, and for a split second I actually thought it might be the source of all this enshrouding silence. It, I swear it seemed to call out to me, *Open the door and step inside.*

WOMAN: Right! And then we heard a noise...

MAN: I turned around to see what it was, but I couldn't see anything. The sun was setting, darkness encroaching. And when I turned back to tell you not to worry, you weren't there. Only your footsteps remained imprinted on the soft ground. A trail I was able to follow right to the front door of the mysterious building. The door was slightly ajar. I called out to you, but you never responded. I rushed inside, but I couldn't find you anywhere. There were no footprints inside the building. Where did you go? (*Pause.*) What did you do there? (*Pause.*) Why won't you answer me?

# PSYCHIATRIST'S PSYCHIATRIST

# THE CHARACTERS

DR. DAVID MURPHY – A man in his 20s.
DISTRESSED WOMAN – A woman of 30.

# THE SCENE

A psychiatrist's office.

*A sparsely decorated room with a well-used couch, some paintings and a few diplomas hung on the walls, a single window with a view of the cityscape/concrete jungle and a desk behind which sits the psychiatrist, DR. DAVID MURPHY.*

*His youthfulness sticks out like a sore thumb. Sitting at his desk, he is absentmindedly reading some papers when he is interrupted by the slightly older DISTRESSED WOMAN who barges inside his office unannounced and without a proper appointment.*

DR. DAVID MURPHY: (*Sits up. Startled.*) Can I help you?

DISTRESSED WOMAN: Well, that's what I am here to find out.

DR. DAVID MURPHY: I am glad you came

to me for help. But please keep in mind for any future sessions, two of my biggest pet peeves happen to be self-assurance and individuals barging in without properly scheduled appointments. What if I was with a patient?

DISTRESSED WOMAN: It doesn't seem like you get too many clients.

DR. DAVID MURPHY: What makes you say that?

DISTRESSED WOMAN: (*She looks around the office.*) Well... there's no receptionist. You are the only person here. (*Pause.*) And why don't you like self-assurance? It's an admirable quality. Barging in I can understand, although I was raised in a family that considers showing up on time better left to the low earning wage dependant working class who can't stand to lose a minute.

DR. DAVID MURPHY: I am used to women lacking assertiveness, distressed women on the brink of suicide who have a hard time finding my office. (*Pause.*) And preferably well-mannered ones that knock before they enter.

DISTRESSED WOMAN: (*Shrugs.*) Oh well, I can assure you that I am very suicidal. (*She begins to pace the office, pausing to look at the diplomas and the cheap paintings.*) I just want to make sure you are the right fit for me before I fall apart on your comfy couch.

DR. DAVID MURPHY: Was the last psychiatrist the wrong fit?

DISTRESSED WOMAN, *mysteriously*: Well, you could say that.

DR. DAVID MURPHY: Is that what YOU would say?

DISTRESSED WOMAN: (*She approaches the window; it is dirty and smudged. Her hands grip the bottom, and with great effort she gets it to slide up. She leans halfway out and looks down.*) I would say he was the WRONG FIT. I mean, what else can one say about a man who jumps out of a twelfth-story window, shatters all over the sidewalk below and leaves behind a big puddle of blood.

DR. DAVID MURPHY: That sounds horrific.

DISTRESSED WOMAN, *wickedly*: No, the horrific part was the blood geyser that splashed innocent children and their cones next to an ice cream truck. (*Pause.*) That might stay with them for a while.

DR. DAVID MURPHY, *confused*: You have an interesting sense of humor.

DISTRESSED WOMAN: All morbid people have that.

DR. DAVID MURPHY: Maybe you should try your hand at stand-up comedy.

DISTRESSED WOMAN: I would rather not drive people to commit suicide.

DR. DAVID MURPHY: You just want to commit it yourself.

DISTRESSED WOMAN, *thoughtfully*: Maybe and maybe not. What I didn't want was to remain stagnant and do absolutely nothing. Just me, myself and I locked away in a glass cage waiting for a rock to shatter my existence.

DR. DAVID MURPHY: So, you reached out for help.

DISTRESSED WOMAN: Or so I thought I did. Until... (*Pause.*)

DR. DAVID MURPHY: Your therapist jumped. (*Pause.*) It must have come as such a shock to receive that call.

DISTRESSED WOMAN: Oh, there was no call. He jumped in front of me.

DR. DAVID MURPHY: You mean...?

DISTRESSED WOMAN: Yes, we were having a session.

DR. DAVID MURPHY: And what did he say?

DISTRESSED WOMAN: "I need to get some fresh air." He walked to the window, opened it, and climbed out.

DR. DAVID MURPHY, *incredulously*: Did he look back at you?

DISTRESSED WOMAN: Yes, he did. He was smiling.

DR. DAVID MURPHY: He smiled?

DISTRESSED WOMAN: Smiled and then winked.

DR. DAVID MURPHY: He winked at you? You sure it was not just something in his eye?

DISTRESSED WOMAN: No, he definitely winked at me.

DR. DAVID MURPHY: I wonder what it meant.

DISTRESSED WOMAN: I don't think there's any subtext to it. He just winked. I mean, the whole thing was sort of funny.

DR. DAVID MURPHY: (*Shakes his head.*) He must have been stressed out with his practice and patients and literally gone to pieces over his work.

DISTRESSED WOMAN: His body was remarkably whole, albeit a bit pancake-like. (*Pause.*) And I highly doubt it was his work considering I was his only patient.

DR. DAVID MURPHY: His only patient?

DISTRESSED WOMAN: Well, after he took up my case and we started to sleep together, he dropped everyone else. He told me no one mattered except me.

DR. DAVID MURPHY: You were sleeping with him?

DISTRESSED WOMAN: Is that so uncommon? I almost always thought of it as a job perk in this profession.

DR. DAVID MURPHY: I can reassure you that not all of us sleep with our patients.

DISTRESSED WOMAN, *smilingly*: If you actually had patients. I am sure you would want to.

DR. DAVID MURPHY, *helplessly*: I... (*Pause.*)

DISTRESSED WOMAN: Come on, Doc, can you imagine sniveling, vulnerable women with low-cut dresses laying on your couch all day long telling you their innermost secrets, putting you in a position of power over them. You are telling me that wouldn't get your dick hard?

DR. DAVID MURPHY: (*Nervously coughs.*) My penis should not be of any concern to you at this moment.

DISTRESSED WOMAN: Well, Doc, for now, you can keep it to yourself. I am sure eventually it will pop out during one of our future sessions. They always do. (*She winks at him.*) I like you. You can consider me your first official patient. Just don't jump on me. Remember, I'm the one with the issues. (*She walks out of the office.*)

# CLASS DISTINCTIONS

# THE CHARACTERS

YOUNG WOMAN – A woman in her 20s.
HOMELESS YOUTH – A man in his 20s.

# THE SCENE

A subway station.

*A busy subway station. People rushing to their destinations at a maddening pace with no regard for anyone else's personal space.*

HOMELESS YOUTH, 20-something, disheveled and hungry, is sitting on the floor of the station watching this human traffic pass him by. There is a hat with a few coins next to his feet.

YOUNG WOMAN, urbanite, eloquent in her movements but with an intense gaze, catches his eye when she tries to walk past without acknowledging him.

HOMELESS YOUTH, *challengingly*: You don't have a heart.

YOUNG WOMAN: (*She stops, taken aback by*

*his direct approach.*) Excuse me?

HOMELESS YOUTH, *persistently*: I said... you don't have a heart.

YOUNG WOMAN: If I didn't have a beating heart, I wouldn't be alive right now, standing here talking to you.

HOMELESS YOUTH, *cockily*: That's not the kind of heart I was talking about.

YOUNG WOMAN: So not the physical but the spiritual type, right? The kind that's capable of things like compassion, sympathy and empathy.

HOMELESS YOUTH: That's exactly the type I was talking about. (*Pause.*) So knowing all this, why do you pass me every day, Monday to Friday, and have never once found it in yourself to spare me some change? (*Pause.*) All you do is give me that long glance as you walk past. That's why I said you don't have a heart.

YOUNG WOMAN: Because I acknowledge

you but don't find myself reaching into my purse for money that I slave for every single day to just hand over to you for what... just sitting there?

HOMELESS YOUTH: That's exactly right.

YOUNG WOMAN: (*She laughs from sheer disbelief.*) You have some nerve. Do you ever stop and think about anyone but yourself? The world doesn't revolve around you just because you are sitting on the floor of a subway station begging for change in the financial district of the city.

HOMELESS YOUTH: And what about you? Strutting around like you're on a catwalk. This isn't a fashion show. You walk around like you own it all.

YOUNG WOMAN: Own what? The subway platform? I think the city owns that.

HOMELESS YOUTH: A wisecracking privileged girl wearing a designer coat...

(*She interrupts him.*)

YOUNG WOMAN: You still haven't told me

what I own. What exactly is that in your opinion? Please clue me in about my supposed riches.

HOMELESS YOUTH: You own this. (*He gesticulates all around him.*) All this! (*Pause.*) Entitlement is a disease that infects many. You are clearly a victim of it.

YOUNG WOMAN: And you are clearly a victim of bad choices and poverty. But that's obvious. What isn't so obvious is why you're channelling a terrible car salesman, trying so desperately hard to sell me something without paying an iota of attention to my needs as a customer... which in this case is to leave the showroom and get on with my day.

HOMELESS YOUTH: What is it that I am trying to sell you exactly?

YOUNG WOMAN: You are selling an idea. You prey on strong, successful women, and then you attack them for being strong and having money. You pick away at their confidence to bring them down a few notches, just so you can make them feel guilty for being where they are. For having what they have. You are selling the idea of *YOU*.

HOMELESS YOUTH: People around here have money to spare. They sure make enough of it.

YOUNG WOMAN: And you want some of it. But just because someone dresses nicely or walks a certain way doesn't necessarily mean they have money. Some do, and some don't. People from all walks of life and social classes are willing to contribute. Some more readily than others. The ones that aren't so quick to give had probably asked themselves a very good question: What will the money purchase? (*Pause.*) So, what will you purchase with that money?

HOMELESS YOUTH: (*He grimaces. His face deformed by anger.*) That's none of your business!

YOUNG WOMAN: (*She smiles broadly.*) It's

my money. That makes it my business.

HOMELESS YOUTH: Not once you have handed it over.

YOUNG WOMAN: But have I handed it over? I haven't, have I? (*Pause.*) I want you to broaden your horizons, expand your mind beyond the beggar's mentality, past the one-way transaction of a perfectly capable individual who shuns employment to freeload. Start looking at it from a business perspective. It's a donation that comes with a price.

HOMELESS YOUTH: (*He spits on the ground over his left shoulder.*) Good old upper classes and their fucked-up legislature. So, tell me, what's the price?

YOUNG WOMAN: An assurance that you won't senselessly spend the money. Convince me. Clarify the end destination. Intended purpose for my contribution. If I had to guess, a liquor store. Or drugs that you'd administer hopefully at a safe injection site. Cigarettes, booze, and drugs. The nourishment of the destitute and the broken. (*Pause.*) So, are you going to tell me? Or do I just go on guessing? It's the only way to get me to reach inside my purse and give you something.

HOMELESS YOUTH, *defensively*: I don't have to do anything.

YOUNG WOMAN: I can see that. Why would you? You have retired; you yearn for nothing having acquired all those worldly possessions you coveted in your earlier years, through your perseverance and hard work you are now living comfortably in a spacious outmoded house. Of course, you no longer have to do anything. (*She smiles ruthlessly.*) Now if you can accompany me back to reality for a moment. I get it, maybe you haven't taken any business courses, but this is a business transaction like any other. Wouldn't you agree?

HOMELESS YOUTH: No, I would not.

YOUNG WOMAN: Really? Because it seems to me that we both want something from one another. Look, I know you can't afford a financial consultant, so let me give you some advice, free of charge. People like knowing where their money is going, which is what your beggar's sign seems to be lacking. I have a marker on me. If you want, we can add that in right now. Of course, you'd have to tell me what it is that you are going to do with this cash, which brings us right back to where we started.

HOMELESS YOUTH: (*He laughs.*) Cash... people barely spare change. You're telling me if I tell you what I will use this money for, you'll give me more than just change.

YOUNG WOMAN: You'd be surprised what people are willing do for others if they truly believe in their intentions.

HOMELESS YOUTH: You haven't answered my question.

YOUNG WOMAN: It would have to be something I believe in.

HOMELESS YOUTH: So, there's a catch.

YOUNG WOMAN: Everything in life comes with a catch. There's no such thing as free money.

HOMELESS YOUTH: What about the people who give me whatever change they have and walk away without even waiting for a thank you?

YOUNG WOMAN: A guilty conscience can be a strong persuader.

HOMELESS YOUTH: Which is something you don't seem to suffer from.

YOUNG WOMAN: You are right; I don't. I didn't get to where I am by walking over corpse-strewn sidewalks; my conscience is untroubled. When I donate, I donate out of the goodness of my heart, not because of some terrible pangs of guilt. I donate because I care, not because I am trying to purchase a first-class ticket to heaven through carefully calculated financial contributions.

HOMELESS YOUTH: No, you clearly got there by being a frigid, greedy, and all-around judgmental bitch.

YOUNG WOMAN: Well, that's why I am wearing Christian Louboutin leather pumps and you... have bags wrapped around your feet. That's a pretty clear distinction if I ever seen one painted so vividly. So, are you going to tell me about your intentions, or should I go?

HOMELESS YOUTH, *barely audible*: Fuck-ing bitch.

YOUNG WOMAN: What was that?!

HOMELESS YOUTH: Nothing... so you want to know about my intentions.

YOUNG WOMAN: Yes, dying to hear about those.

HOMELESS YOUTH: I would use the money to get some food to help me concentrate as I flip through the classifieds looking for a job.

YOUNG WOMAN: Funny... the scars on

your arm tell a different story. People lie, track marks unerringly record the truth. You can't refute an accurately kept record jotted down one prick at a time.

(*The Homeless Youth rolls down his sleeves.*)

YOUNG WOMAN: A piece of advice. Switch to a cheaper drug of choice. Try crack. More affordable and you might even have some leftover change to buy yourself some food.

HOMELESS YOUTH: What is your fucking problem?!

YOUNG WOMAN: I don't have a problem. You seem to be the one with the problem. My wallet is actually quite full. You are the one with lint in his pockets. I am just trying to help you out with some sound advice.

HOMELESS YOUTH: I don't want your sound advice; I want your fucking money, lady.

YOUNG WOMAN: I know you do. But if you want my money, you must earn it. And being a demanding junkie is not the best way to go about it. Anyone ever teach you manners when you were younger?

HOMELESS YOUTH: What do you know about my upbringing?

YOUNG WOMAN: I never said I did but spare me what comes next. I don't want to hear your sappy story about not having parents and being stuck in a foster home, and this is exactly why you ended up here today. I don't care. What I care about is what you are doing now, today, tomorrow, about getting off these streets.

HOMELESS YOUTH: And what about you, miss perfect? What's your drug of choice? A glass of wine every night before bed? Maybe the whole bottle?

YOUNG WOMAN: I don't drink.

HOMELESS YOUTH: Everyone drinks.

YOUNG WOMAN: I don't. My parents were alcoholics.

HOMELESS YOUTH: At least you had parents.

YOUNG WOMAN: What did I tell you about sappy stories from your past? I don't care. You look hurt. I have some tissues in my purse next to my wallet if you want to wipe away those tears in your eyes.

HOMELESS YOUTH: Fuck You!

YOUNG WOMAN: I don't usually fuck unemployed men. I do have some standards. Hey, I have an idea. Let's try to find you a job and then you can maybe ask me out. No guarantees I will say yes.

HOMELESS YOUTH: Do you know how many people die out here every day because of heartless people like you?

YOUNG WOMAN: I don't think anyone dies in the actual station. They die out there. In the streets.

HOMELESS YOUTH: What difference does that make!

YOUNG WOMAN: I don't know. I've just always been a stickler for details, which is why you currently aren't in possession of my money.

HOMELESS YOUTH: Fuck you!

YOUNG WOMAN: We have already been over this. The answer is still no. Cheer up! You are young. You aren't suffering from schizophrenia, and life expectancy for a homeless person is around thirty-nine years. Still a long time to go before you die. It's a gradual process. Don't sweat it, bud. You will live to see tomorrow and put in another solid appearance at your job as a professional panhandler.

HOMELESS YOUTH, *angrily*: I seriously want to kick your teeth in.

YOUNG WOMAN: Violence is never the answer. But since you seem to be having such a tough time with donations toward your very charitable cause, I would suggest you pack up for the day and go to a shelter. A warm bed and a meal usually beat a cold marble floor.

HOMELESS YOUTH: Do you know what it costs to keep a youth in a shelter? Thirty to forty grand a year.

YOUNG WOMAN: That sounds about right. What's your point? Where are you heading with this?

HOMELESS YOUTH: Lack of available spots. That's where I was heading with this.

YOUNG WOMAN: I am going to call your bluff and pull your card. Are you seriously trying to tell me that every single shelter in this city is at full capacity? If one is full, you try another one.

HOMELESS YOUTH: And how do you expect me to know whether they are full or not?

YOUNG WOMAN: Ever heard of that nifty Alexander Graham Bell invention called the telephone? There's a payphone right outside this station; all you need is some change... (*She looks down at his hat on the ground.*) ...which I see you already have.

HOMELESS YOUTH: What made you such a cold analytical realist?

YOUNG WOMAN: Life in general. Also living on the streets, begging for money, and sleeping in shelters. You don't remember me, Sam, but we used to sit on corners side by side cuddling together for body heat. Just us against the savage elements of an indifferent society.

HOMELESS YOUTH: (*He slowly processes the information, slack-jawed, shocked.*) Chrissy?

YOUNG WOMAN: I see your memory is still intact. It just needed some prodding.

HOMELESS YOUTH: How did you...

YOUNG WOMAN: I got help, Sam. Shelters can be amazing at connecting you with the right people. All you have to want is something more than a handout. (*She reaches in her purse and offers him a card.*

# CHRISTINE BIRDWELL.

# SHELTER DEPUTY MANAGER.)

*A big thank you to Oliviaprodesign for her amazing work crafting the cover of this book. And another special thank you to Lee D. Thompson for his editorial and typesetting services. A brilliant editor, an amazing writer, and a genuine friend.*

*Additionally, I want to thank Noah Clemons (author, YouTube Channel: Everyone Who Reads it Must Converse) and Phillip Freedenberg (author of* America and the Cult of the Cactus Boots) *for their consistent support of my work.*

*Last but not least, a special thank you to Joseph McElroy. Our brief correspondence served as true inspiration.*